He thou

Yet he hadn't considered that she had a ripe figure under those boxy suits she'd always worn. Hadn't guessed her laughter was so husky and stimulating, or that her smile could do things to…

A tightening in his gut caused his grin to fade. He gripped the metal rail. Peabody was not a woman to him. She was more than that. Women were replaceable. Peabody was essential. She had a good, sharp mind and ran his office like a top sergeant.

"I will not mess up a perfect working relationship simply because her laugh…"

He turned around and propped a hip against the railing. The bed snagged his gaze. He eyed the thing, concerned. He'd had every intention of platonically sharing that puny mattress with Peabody. The idea of anything physical going on between them had no more entered his head than if he'd planned to sleep beside his briefcase.

Until now.

Renee Roszel has been writing romance novels since 1983 and simply loves her job. She likes to keep her stories humorous and light, with her heroes gorgeous, sexy and larger than life. She says, "Why not spend your days and nights with the very best!" Luckily for Renee, her husband is gorgeous and sexy, too!

Praise for Renee Roszel:

"Renee Roszel creates wonderful characters who will walk off the page and into your heart."
—*Romantic Times*

"She is delightful, eloquent and humorous all in one."
—*Rendezvous*

Books by Renee Roszel

Don't miss any of our special offers. Write to us at the following address for information on our newest releases.

Harlequin Reader Service
U.S.: 3010 Walden Ave., P.O. Box 1325, Buffalo, NY 14269
Canadian: P.O. Box 609, Fort Erie, Ont. L2A 5X3

The One-Week Marriage
Renee Roszel

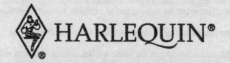

TORONTO • NEW YORK • LONDON
AMSTERDAM • PARIS • SYDNEY • HAMBURG
STOCKHOLM • ATHENS • TOKYO • MILAN • MADRID
PRAGUE • WARSAW • BUDAPEST • AUCKLAND

To my aunts
Eva and Anna May,
women of humor and quiet strength

ISBN 0-373-03559-4

THE ONE-WEEK MARRIAGE

First North American Publication 1999.

Copyright © 1999 by Renee Roszel Wilson.

Look us up on-line at: http://www.romance.net

Printed in U.S.A.

CHAPTER ONE

"MR. PARISH, you really must choose a wife, today."
Izzy Peabody dropped a leather-bound catalog on her
boss's desk. It landed on the polished walnut with a
sharp crack. She wasn't happy about his plan and she
didn't care if he knew it. After all, she was quitting,
wasn't she? Hadn't she been carrying her resignation
letter around in her purse for a month? All she had
to do was work up her courage to hand it to him.

"What did you say, Peabody?" Gabriel Parish
shouted from the private bathroom in his Manhattan
office. He stuck his head out the door and Izzy sucked
in an appreciative breath. It didn't seem to matter how
many times she'd seen him in exactly that pose—half
shaved and shirtless, his upper torso and broad shoulders displaying delectable muscle—the sight always
shook her to her core. Without fear of contradiction,
Izzy knew that within the six-foot-three-inch hunk
that was Gabriel Parish, any woman would find her
fantasy man.

Black tousled hair fell across his forehead as his
emerald gaze shifted to fix on her, full of professional
curiosity and nothing more. It was agonizing for Izzy
to be continually reminded that Mr. Parish didn't
think of her as anything but his faithful right arm—
his "Peabody"—not a living, breathing woman who
had foolishly fallen in love with her boss.

"I said, you really must take a minute to pick your
wife," she called, grateful she sounded composed.

"My what?" Those breathtaking eyes widened a fraction. She might have smiled at his dubious reaction, if it didn't make her so miserable. Mr. Parish actually picking out a wife was a ludicrous notion. He had no desire to marry. And why should he, with a continual flow of gorgeous women simpering and wiggling through his life?

Trying to keep on track, she hefted the black catalog. "For the Yum-Yum account. Remember?"

From his quick, disgruntled frown, it was clear that he did. "Oh, right." Disappearing into his bathroom, he shouted, "In a minute."

She turned to go.

"Peabody, I forgot a shirt. Would you bring me a fresh one?"

She halted, wincing. That's all she needed. To be forced into close proximity with the man's chest. "Right away, Mr. Parish," she said thinly, pivoting toward the quarters he used for his home away from home. When business—or social—engagements went too late for him to return to his Long Island estate, he slept in his office apartment.

Evidently last night had been one of those late nights. Entering the expensively appointed bedroom, she couldn't help but notice that his bed was rumpled. She tried not to visualize possible reasons he stayed here last night—or arrived very early—since she knew he hadn't been entertaining advertising clients. *Besides,* she reminded herself sternly, *it's none of your business what Mr. Parish does after hours!*

Grabbing a fresh shirt from the dresser, she returned through his office to the bathroom. The door stood ajar, but she knocked, hoping not to have to face him until he was fully clothed. "I have the shirt."

"Well, bring it in."

She eyed heaven. What had she done to deserve this? "Yes, sir."

He patted his face dry with a thick, white towel. Izzy inhaled and was struck broadside with his scent, so stirringly male. She swallowed hard, making herself breathe in shallow sniffs to keep his essence out of her head.

The bathroom was large with white marble on walls, countertops, even the floor. Golden faucets, handles and towel racks gleamed as only real gold could.

On the wall above the sink, a large mirror reflected her and her boss in unrelenting brightness. Unfortunately his image was not compromised in the slightest by light that should have exposed every flaw. The stark brilliance emphasized the firm sensuality of his mouth, the glossy blackness of his hair, those devilishly thick lashes and the gemlike quality of his green eyes. Her glance trailed down. When she discovered where her wanderings had taken her, she focused on his chin, warning herself not to stare at his chest. Her heart could only stand so much.

He flung the towel over a nearby rack, the act setting off a bothersome play of muscle in shoulder and arm. He grasped the shirt she held. She hardly noticed until he gave it a little jerk. "Peabody?" he asked. "Are you with me?"

She blinked and let go. "Why don't you bring in that catalog? We can go over the candidates now and get it done before my eight o'clock meeting with Baxter Sports Equipment."

Izzy nodded, her glance fastened on the golden faucet for safety's sake. "Yes, sir," she murmured, turning away. She had no more desire to idle in the bathroom with Mr. Parish than she did to watch him nuzzle the neck of some svelte socialite. With a sudden thought, she faced him. "Unless you'd rather do it at lunch when you have more time to—"

"No," he cut in. "Let's get my wife firmed up."

As she headed for his desk she almost smiled at the irony. "I don't imagine any wife you'd choose would need much firming up," she mumbled, grabbing the Celestial Companion and Chaperon catalog, containing employee photographs and vital statistics.

Celestial was a highly regarded New York firm, providing purely respectable escorts. Even so, the idea of her employer hiring somebody to *pretend* to be his wife—for a trip to a private, tropical island— didn't sound all that pure or respectable. Where Mr. Parish was concerned, not many women who spent time in his company seemed concerned about keeping a relationship with him particularly pure *or* respectable.

She winced at the visions that barged into her mind. *"I have to quit this job!"* she muttered.

Upon reentering the bathroom, she was only slightly relieved to see that he'd slid on the shirt. It wasn't buttoned. With a curt nod, he indicated the marble counter. "Lay it there so I can look while I finish dressing."

She did so, her jaws clamped tight. *Keep your eyes on the pictures,* she admonished silently, but her wayward gaze drifted to his reflection—and his chest.

"Nothing interesting there. Turn the page."

She jumped and did as he commanded, relieved to

notice the next time her errant glance traveled to his reflection he was buttoning the shirt.

"Nothing there, either, Peabody." The mellow sound of her name glanced off the walls and echoed in her brain. Peabody—Peabody—*Peabody!* His impersonal tone taunted her, and she reaffirmed her vow to hand him her resignation. Soon! Very soon!

At his bidding, she flipped through a number of pages, each containing four photographs of lovely women, personal information printed under each photo. Izzy didn't know what Mr. Parish might be looking for, but if the ones he'd rejected so far were any indication, he was very choosy. She supposed she shouldn't be surprised. Wasn't he a perfectionist in every aspect of his work? Why shouldn't he be that way even with a wife he would only need for a week?

As she turned another page, her glance caught on her reflection. The harsh lighting was less flattering to her image. She seemed very blah—a blah brown. Her chestnut hair, parted in the middle, was coiled at her nape. Her boxy business suit, a dingy mushroom-colored linen, showed nothing of her figure. Even her eyes were an uninspiring shade of brown. She looked like a common brown wren.

Of course that's how she'd looked for her three years in Mr. Parish's employ. The day she walked in to the outer office to apply for the job, and met the matronly executive assistant who was retiring, Izzy realized that Gabriel Parish was looking for a top-notch aide, not a glamour girl.

She'd looked around the crowded reception room, knowing she had hours to wait before her turn to be interviewed. Unobtrusively she'd slipped out to make herself into the image of what she sensed Mr. Parish wanted. When she returned, gone was the makeup, the youthful-chic attire. She'd even knotted her long, flowing curls at her nape. She looked older than her twenty-three years, efficient and drab.

And now, right this minute, the image in the mirror looked both drab and unhappy—not a good combination for her mental health. Izzy was not by nature either restrained or drab. She'd repressed her true self much too long. Though the money was exceptional as executive assistant to the CEO of Gabriel Parish AdVentures, money wasn't everything. She simply had to get away. *Get a life!*

"Peabody?"

Her gaze darted to his face. "Uh, yes, sir?" He finished knotting his tie, then indicated a photograph. "That redhead. She looks good."

Izzy stared at the woman he indicated. She was breathtaking; exotic bone structure, full, pouty lips bowed in a Mona Lisa smile and enough fiery hair to stuff a couch. There was no getting around the fact that Mr. Parish had an eye for feminine beauty. "Sir..." She cleared a quiver from her throat. "Maybe you should pick out two or three, in case she's not available."

When he didn't immediately respond, she glanced at him, startled to see a knowing smile on his lips. Her heart flip-flopped at the sight. The man had a real talent for grinning. But what was the grin all about? "Did I say something funny?" she asked, sounding foolishly breathless.

"I don't think there'll be a problem." His eyes sparkled with amusement, and Izzy realized he was laughing at her naiveté. For her to even be concerned about the woman's availability was laughable. "Take care of it, Peabody.'' Clapping her on the shoulder in a comradely gesture, he strode out of the bathroom. ''When the Baxter people get here, send them to the conference room, then buzz me.''

Gulping down several breaths, Izzy got her heart rate under control. ''Yes…sir.'' She touched the place on her shoulder where his hand had so recently been. Her boss never doubted for an instant that the stunning redhead would accept his deal.

He was right, of course. He would pay her more for one week's work, pretending to be his wife, than she'd make in a month of dinner and theater dates. Not to mention the wardrobe he planned to purchase for her stay on the island. And last but far from least, he was handsome as sin and a millionaire to boot. There wasn't a woman pictured in the catalog who would refuse his offer. They'd probably agree to go for free.

Realizing she was still massaging the place he'd touched, she dropped her hand, irritated with herself for her stupid preoccupation. Clasping the open volume to her chest, she marched out of the bathroom aiming for the double-doored exit from her boss's high-rise office.

''Oh, and Peabody?'' Reflexively she turned as he came out of his apartment, shrugging on a suit coat. With her efficient-executive-assistant facade in place, she gave him an expectant look. ''Yes, sir?''

''Try to get that disapproving-maiden-aunt expression off your face.''

Heat rose up her cheeks. She'd thought he was oblivious to everything about her except the part that ran his office. *Especially her face.*

She swallowed with difficulty as he settled into the

leather chair behind his desk. A dark brow arched as he continued to eye her. "There's no reason I should be married because a potential client is so eccentric he demands that even the head of his advertising agency be family oriented. That's pure foolishness!"

He lifted a golden pen, shifting toward a stack of papers on his desk. "I can create an excellent advertising campaign as well single as I could married. As a matter of fact, I can do a better job *unmarried*— considering how much trouble women are." He paused to write a word or two then glanced her way. "Right, Peabody?"

Her chin went up at his unintended slap. He didn't think of her as a woman. She prayed he would assume her physical reaction to the slight was a half nod of agreement, rather than pain.

Didn't she know better than anyone—except Mr. Parish, himself—that women on the receiving end of his charm and good manners quickly became jealous and possessive, choosing to believe his attention meant more than it did. Izzy had witnessed too many dreadful scenes right there in the office between females he dated. No wonder he thought women were trouble. To him, they were.

This was exactly why he opted to hire a fake wife rather than give any current lady-love hope that his affections were stronger than they were—or ever would be.

"Well, Peabody?" he asked, breaking through her thoughts. "Don't you have anything to say?"

Yes, I do have something to say, Mr. Parish! she cried mentally. *It's too hard to be close to you day after day—watching you smile that kiss-me-if-you-dare smile, hearing that smoky voice, inhaling that scent that makes me weak, every second knowing you can't see me as any more human than your cellular phone or your fax machine! I quit! I'm leaving—today! Right now! Goodbye and good riddance Mr. Women-Are-Trouble!*

She ground her teeth, wishing she could blurt all that out, throw her resignation letter in his face and stalk out of his life. But gazing into his eyes she couldn't bring herself to do it. And that made her furious with herself. *Coward! Sniveling, cringing, lovesick coward!*

Straightening her shoulders, she eyed him with as much nerve as she could marshal. She didn't like the deception he was planning. Just because Mr. Rufus, the elderly founder of the Yum-Yum Baby Food company, chose to live a reclusive life on his own private island, and would never suspect the lie, was no reason to do this shameful thing.

She eyed her boss narrowly. "Would you like me to rent you a couple of kids, too?" she quipped, trusting her sarcasm said it all.

He watched her for a second without any noticeable reaction to her wisecrack. "No," he said after a heartbeat. "A wife will do." Turning away, he went back to poring over the papers on his desk. "That will be all, Peabody."

Dismissed, she wheeled around to escape. Her flight across the plush, jade carpet created no sound; her sensible pumps hardly made an impression. The irony galled. Even his carpet hardly registered her presence. As for Mr. Parish, he thought so little of her it didn't occur to him that she even had the capacity to crack a joke.

Of course, neither did his cell phone or his fax machine.

Thirteen days after Mr. Parish chose the beautiful redhead, Miss Dawn Day, to be his fake wife, it was time to put the fraud into action.

Sunday morning, May 3, Izzy and her boss stood in La Guardia's TransGlobal First Class lounge. Any other time the room would have had a relaxing influence, decorated in earth tones, leather and luxuriant green plants. But today, it was obvious that Mr. Parish saw none of it.

"She's late." He scowled at his watch. "Did you send James with the limo?"

"Yes, sir." Izzy closed her notebook, hoping he was through giving orders for the coming week. "I'm sure they'll be along any second." She started to put her notebook inside her shoulder bag, then hesitated, glancing at him. "Any other instructions, sir?"

He regarded her with a disgruntled frown. "Did you say something, Peabody?"

"I said, will there be any other instructions?"

"Oh." His jaw worked. "No." He shifted to check the door of the lounge. Almost unforgivably, it remained closed.

Izzy opened her purse and deposited her notebook inside. Her hand brushed her resignation letter and she bit down on the inside of her cheek. For the millionth time since she'd written the thing she was racked with indecision. Her fingers curled around the envelope. *Now would be a good time to give it to him,* her logical side urged. *He'd have a week away from you to get accustomed to the idea. He probably wouldn't even be cross when he returned.*

"What about her ticket?"

Izzy jumped, yanking her hand from her purse as though it held a poisonous snake. "Um, uh, I sent it by messenger. She got it. I called and checked."

Gabriel Parish scowled and Izzy was captured by the picture he made standing there before the large window. He glanced down. Morning sun glinted off the tips of his long eyelashes, then flashed off the gold of his Rolex as he snapped up his wrist.

In an expensive ebony suit and bold black-and-white striped tie, he exuded self-confident masculinity—a sight that would make any female heart flutter. The furtive peeks of other women in the lounge went unnoticed by her boss, heedless of everything except his immediate concerns. But they were glaringly apparent to Izzy. Masking a dejected sigh, she snapped her purse shut. Once again, she couldn't bring herself to hand him her resignation letter. Not today.

Movement at the lounge entrance brought Izzy's gaze around to see an incredibly lovely woman burst through the door. Her long, trim legs ate up the distance, even encumbered as she was by impossibly high ankle-strap stilettos. Her chic yellow suit-dress set off her figure and flowing red hair to extraordinary advantage. Izzy's heart sank to some deep pit as her boss's hired wife neared, smiling, her gaze riveted on Mr. Parish. If ever there had been a perfectly matched duo in the world, Dawn Day and Gabriel Parish were that duo. It would be easy to believe they were a couple—both tall, intimidatingly perfect—icons for their gender.

"She's here," Izzy said, appalled at the dejection in her tone.

"Ah, good."

The sound of Mr. Parish's voice drew her gaze to his face. His troubled frown gone, he smiled at the woman. Behind the new arrival trailed James, Mr. Parish's driver. A tiny frown rode his sandy brows, no doubt due to worry that he might be in trouble for getting Miss Day there so late.

The redhead held out a perfectly manicured hand. "Mr. Parish? I'm Dawn Day." Her voice was soft and low, every bit as alluring as her face and figure.

Reaching deep inside herself for the willpower to keep her expression composed, Izzy studied her from a few steps behind her boss.

"I'm sorry about the delay. I had a slight problem, but it's nothing to concern you." She placed a hand on her cheek, then seemed to realize what she'd done and dropped it. Izzy thought the jerky move odd and looked closer at the woman's face.

Mr. Parish took her hand. "It's a pleasure to meet you, Dawn." His smile was so dazzling it could have made angels cry. Obviously he was pleased with what he saw. "You're here. That's what matters."

Dawn smiled again, then winced slightly. Her hand fluttered to her cheek, then darted away.

"Is anything wrong?" Izzy asked, moving to get a closer look.

Dawn's big, blue eyes found Izzy and her smile faltered for a fraction of a second. "Why…no. What could be wrong?" The faintest edge of trepidation in her voice heightened Izzy's concerns.

Dawn shifted her gaze to Mr. Parish. "I have my boarding pass." She held it up. "So all is well."

He lifted it from her fingers, slipping it into his pocket with his own. "It should just be a few minutes." Taking her arm, he added, "Why don't we sit?"

As Mr. Parish led his striking companion toward a seating area that looked more like a man's cushy den than a waiting room, Izzy noticed what appeared to be a slight puffiness along the redhead's otherwise perfect jawline. Once again the woman tentatively touched the place. Izzy had the impression Mr. Parish's fake wife might be in some pain.

James touched Izzy's shoulder. "When do I pick them up again?"

She didn't look his way, but continued to survey Dawn's profile. "A week from today. Five o'clock in the afternoon."

"Should I leave now?"

"Wait until they take off." She glanced at the driver. He was young, nice-looking, new at his job and trying hard. "Once, last year, the plane was taxiing down the runway when something went wrong with the engine and the flight had to be postponed. Mr. Parish doesn't like to dawdle at airports when he can go work at his office for a few hours. So, never leave until the plane disappears into the distance."

James nodded, looking solemn.

She smiled at him, feeling for the young man. Their employer could be intimidating. Touching James's hand in a friendly gesture, she added, "If you have questions, ask me." As soon as the words were out of her mouth, she was sorry. Ask me? *How could you have said such a thing, dummy?* she admonished inwardly. *Remember, you're quitting!*

The chauffeur's frown evaporated and he looked almost at ease. She supposed her tiny fib was worth it if she reduced James's stress level. He was a wiry, high-strung man, taking everything too seriously.

"I don't think that lady feels good," James whispered.

Izzy had gone back to studying Dawn's face, so the chauffeur's remark snagged her attention. "I was thinking the same thing."

"She kept touching her face and popping aspirin. She spotted me watching her in the rearview mirror and almost snapped my head off. Told me to mind my business and drive."

"Oh, dear." Izzy was beginning to have a bad feeling. The three summers she worked in her father's dentist office hadn't been wasted. Izzy had seen a lot of dental problems walk in the office door. Dawn Day might be an icon of female beauty, but if Izzy didn't miss her guess, behind those ravishing lips lurked trouble. "If she has what I think she has, she's going to need medical attention," Izzy murmured, more to herself than to James.

"If you want my opinion, I think she'd rather die than give up this trip."

Izzy glanced thoughtfully at the chauffeur. She wouldn't blame Miss Day if she'd crawled to the airport on broken arms and legs. Mr. Parish was making it worth any woman's while to take this jaunt. Not to mention the added bonus that *he* would be there. Nevertheless, if the woman had an abscessed tooth, as Izzy suspected, she couldn't go. Abscesses usually made themselves known at an earlier stage than Miss Day's. Though, a few people never realized they had a problem until the swelling began. They might think it was nothing—just a little ache that would pass— but in a few hours the pain would be excruciating.

Miss Day needed a root canal—*today!* Or by tomorrow morning she wouldn't be able to endure the agony, no matter how spectacular the perks.

Mr. Parish's deep laugh rang out, drawing Izzy's gaze. The woman's throaty giggle was almost too far away to detect. But as Izzy watched, the redhead's fingers moved tentatively across her jaw. It was clear her self-prescribed aspirin treatment was doing little good.

Fine, she thought dourly. *This is just fine!* It was too late to hire anybody else from the agency, still Izzy had no choice. She had to confront the woman. If she allowed her to go, she would never forgive herself.

She looked grimly at James. "I have to do something. The poor thing has no idea what she's in for."

He shrugged. "I don't envy you, ma'am. She's not as sweet as she looks. Be careful she doesn't scratch out your eyes for your trouble."

Izzy surveyed the chauffeur narrowly, battling to hold on to a resolve that was trying to scurry into hiding. "Thanks," she quipped wryly. "You're a *huge* help."

Squaring her shoulders, she headed toward her boss and his pretty companion. To keep up her nerve, she told herself this was right. Fate had taken a hand to keep her boss from perpetrating this fraud. Miss Day's abscessed tooth might seem like a calamity now, but it was for the better. *Really!*

Still, how was she going to get Miss Day to admit she was in pain? The redhead had already denied she had any troubles at all.

An idea flashed into Izzy's brain and she walked around between the big leather chairs in which Mr.

Parish and Miss Day were seated. "May I get you anything?" she asked, then pretended to be caught by the sight of something unsightly on the redhead's face. "Oh—there's a smudge..." She drew a clean handkerchief from her purse and skimmed it across Miss Day's puffy jaw. "There—"

A shriek split the air as Dawn lurched from the chair. Stumbling away, her hand went to her jaw. "Why—why you *witch!*" she screamed, her blue eyes filling with tears. *"That hurt!"*

Mr. Parish abruptly stood, his confused gaze going from his hysterical companion to Izzy. "What the hell?"

Dawn moaned, tears spilling from her eyes. "Oh—it *hurts!* That witch did it on *purpose!*"

"Did you pinch her, Peabody?"

"No, sir." Sick at heart, Izzy watched as the redhead crumpled back into her chair. Reduced to a miserable heap, Miss Day covered the lower half of her face with both hands, moaning and rocking back and forth.

Izzy placed a solicitous hand on the woman's shoulder. "I'm so sorry. But you must get that tooth looked at right away."

The redhead glared at Izzy, her eyes glittery and wild. "I'm fine, I tell you! *Mind your own business.*"

"You're ill?" Mr. Parish sat down in the chair next to Dawn, his expression worried.

"I'm afraid she has an abscessed tooth, sir," Izzy said quietly.

"That's not true! You're a *liar!*" Dawn cried, then moaned at the pain her yelling caused. She slumped back, her face ashen.

"We're ready to board, Mr. Parish."

Izzy's gaze shot to the newcomer. An attractive flight attendant stood nearby, her features closed in concern.

"May I be of help?" she asked.

Mr. Parish stood. Frowning, he shook his head. "We can manage." He motioned to James. When the chauffeur scurried up, his boss indicated Miss Day. "Drive her to my dentist. His private number is programmed into the car phone."

"But it's Sunday, sir," James said.

"He's a close friend. He'll see her." Solemnly he offered the redhead his hand. "I'm disappointed, Dawn. But I can't allow you to make the trip in your condition."

Slouched dejectedly in the big chair, she looked at him, her eyes awash with pleading and suffering. "I—I need this job."

Izzy watched her boss's jaw harden, a clear indication that he was as disturbed as she. He bent to take her fingers in his. "I'll compensate you for your trouble, Miss Day. Now see about that tooth."

When Mr. Parish helped her to her feet, he handed her over to James and sent them on their way.

The first-class passengers began boarding. Izzy stared at her boss, watching him watch his counterfeit wife disappear—along with his chance at the Yum-Yum Baby Food account. So tall and grim, he was a striking vision, even in defeat.

Although Izzy had been against this ploy from the beginning, she felt a twinge of sadness. Her boss had gone to incredible lengths to get the account. Seeing his chance walk out the door along with Miss Day had to be excruciating. "I—I'm sure you'll realize that—in the long run—this is best, sir."

He shifted to glower at her. He was furious. Gabriel Parish wasn't a man who took kindly to losing. He lived for the stimulation of the quest and reveled in conquest. The money he made was a mere by-product. Mr. Parish had to be suffering the tortures of the damned, seeing this challenge slip through his fingers.

A part of her rejoiced that her boss would not be traveling to an idyllic tropical island with Dawn Day, and she felt a pinch of guilt. Well, fate had spoken. It was time to move on.

She cleared her throat, forcing herself to meet his angry gaze. "I'll see about getting your bags off the plane, sir, but I'm not sure if—"

"*No.*" He grasped her elbow. "Peabody, *you* are going to be my wife for a week."

CHAPTER TWO

His wife?

It wasn't as though she'd never had that fantasy.

But for only a week?

It seemed Mr. Parish and Madam Fate had something in common that Izzy would never have anticipated. Both had a genius for diabolical pranks. Suddenly she had the very thing she'd fantasized about for so long—Gabriel Parish as her husband—yet she didn't really have him at all.

By the time the shock of being dragged onto the plane wore off, Izzy and her boss were thirty thousand feet above the Eastern seaboard, winging south toward Miami. From her window seat, she blinked, coming fully back to reality. She glowered at the man beside her. He was on the phone. His deep chuckle filled the cabin. Izzy saw people turn and smile. His laughter was contagious. People around him caught it like the flu—only with more palatable results.

However, there was nothing palatable going on from where Izzy sat. She had a feeling she was the only person in the half-filled first-class section who wasn't smiling. As her boss talked business with one of his advertising clients, he happened to catch sight of her frown and winked nonchalantly. As if he thought *that* would make it all better! How dare he drag her onto a plane, without even a toothbrush, expecting her to spend the week *lying* for him.

He hung up. "Okay, Peabody," he said, drawing

her glance. "I know you're not crazy about this." She opened her mouth, but he held up a hand, halting her. "Neither am I, but we can make this work." He shifted to better see her. "Don't forget, you're getting a new wardrobe out of the deal, and I'll pay double overtime." His grin was sunny, meant to charm the daylights out of her.

But to Izzy that smile was pure cruelty. He knew no flesh-and-blood woman could withstand it—fiendish, manipulative beast! However, since he didn't think of Izzy as a woman, she had no plans to quiver and sigh and melt like one. Lifting her chin, she muttered, "It didn't cross your mind that I believe this ruse is unfair and that I might refuse to have anything to do with it?"

His smile didn't dim, but somehow became wry. She realized the change was in his eyes, which narrowed slightly. "It crossed my mind."

"And then flitted right out?"

"Yes."

She eyed heaven and turned toward the window. Outside the sun shone on fluffy clouds below them, the image of a snow-covered landscape in some arctic wonderland. "You take me for granted, Mr. Parish," she said. "I don't like that trait in you."

"Are you bucking for a raise, Peabody?" Amusement rode his words.

She twisted to scowl at him. "Everything is *not* about money, sir."

"Reverse psychology." He nodded. "Good strategy. What about five percent?"

She gaped, anger welling inside her. *"What?"*

He chuckled. "Okay, seven."

With an exasperated moan she lay back and closed

her eyes. "I don't want a raise, Mr. Parish. I simply can't abide the idea of lying to that nice man."

"If you like him, you'll go along with my plan."

She peered at him from behind her lashes. "Excuse me?"

"He needs me, Peabody." Mr. Parish leaned closer. Reflexively she fumbled for the controls, pressing her seat back to recline. With her retreat, his grin grew crooked. "There, you see? You're acting like a wife, already."

She frowned. "Your attitude about marriage *alone* should disqualify you!"

"My attitude about marriage shouldn't come into it."

"Well I shouldn't be *here,* but I am." She wasn't sure if her argument held a scrap of logic. With Mr. Parish leaning over her, his face inches above hers, her brain was misfiring. Frantically she pressed her seat button, but nothing happened. She was as far back as she could go.

"Are you telling me life isn't fair, Peabody, and that we must play the hand we're dealt?"

She had no idea if that's what she meant, but decided it sounded good and nodded.

The humor in his expression reminded her of a father tolerating a pampered child. "You don't think I'm playing the hand I was dealt?"

"Yes, I do," she retorted. "But they used to shoot cardsharps for playing a hand the way you're playing yours."

"You think I'm cheating?"

"Think?" She was amazed he could even ask the question.

"I'm not, Peabody. I can't."

"No?" She eyed him with distrust, curious to see how he thought he could weasel out of admitting he was a scoundrel. "I doubt that."

His grin was cocky and sexy. "You can embezzle from a company and cheat on a spouse, Peabody. There are as many ways to cheat as there are people. But you can't cheat on inspiration." He watched her speculatively. "Quality can't be faked. Married or not, I'll give old Rufus quality work." He nudged her, a brief, teasing gesture. "Tell me honestly, do you believe I have any intention of cheating the man?"

She stared at him. *How did he do it?* Deep down, she knew if he got the Yum-Yum account, he would work a miracle—conceive a campaign that would elevate baby food above the mundane and make the hawking of it an earth-shattering event.

Gabriel Parish was gifted that way. She'd seen it happen too many times to doubt his ability. It was almost scary. Defeat washed over her, and she opened her mouth to admit he was right. He wasn't cheating, wouldn't cheat. He was merely playing his hand—his own way. His motto was Nothing Ventured, Nothing Gained and this was simply another venture to him. The method be damned.

Yet, in a sudden flash of insight she couldn't make the admission. *Wouldn't.* No matter how pretty the words he used to justify it, he would still be lying about being married, and she would have to join him in his lie. Forcing herself, she met his gaze. She had to be firm. "I won't do it, Mr. Parish."

He watched her for a minute, his nearness making her too aware of him. The seconds dragged by.

She glared.

He smiled.

She grew panicky. If she looked into those eyes for another second she would agree to anything he asked. "Would you..." She swallowed to ease the tightness in her throat. "Would you back off, sir?"

One dark eyebrow rose a trifle. He turned away to steeple his fingers before his face. He seemed to fall into deep thought. Izzy wondered about what.

Her boss had a keen, unorthodox mind. At thirty-five, he was called "the young genius of promoting" in New York's fast-paced advertising world. His career was his family, his passion, his children, his wife and his love. In the three years she'd been part of his breakneck-take-no-prisoners world she'd never complained, never objected. She had a feeling he wouldn't take her rejection well. *She was tampering with his whole existence.*

Staring out her window, she heaved a sigh. Quite possibly she wouldn't have to hand him her resignation letter after all.

Renewed yearning swelled in her breast. If Mr. Parish only knew how badly she wanted to be his wife. His real wife. Someone he loved, someone he could come to for comfort and happiness. But a sham wife? She couldn't go through with it—being near him, braving false endearments and displays of affection.

The idea was too painful to bear.

She breathed deeply in an effort to remain composed. This was no time for silly tears. After staring out the window for what seemed to be a hundred years, it began to nag her that Mr. Parish continued to say nothing. Her nerves tightened like overwound clock springs, and she felt close to screaming. Why didn't he just say, "You're fired!" and get it over and done? She wanted to look at him, gauge his expression, his posture, his demeanor, but she didn't have the nerve.

After ten more agonizing minutes, she knew if she didn't do something she would jump up and start screaming. That sort of behavior would only get her sent to a home for the mentally disturbed or a cell in airline prison.

She peeked at her boss. It startled her to see that he'd reclined his seat and appeared to be sleeping. *Sleeping?* The sight did unruly things to her. His hawk-like features were riveting and seductive, even in repose.

But sleeping? This wasn't the way she'd expected her driven, aggressive boss to react. She'd expected reasoning, cajoling and endless charm—until she finally surrendered, a trembling, simpering nitwit. It was out of character for him to give up. And he never napped on trips. He always had his briefcase open, working on his pitch. Baffled, she leaned toward him and waved a hand over his eyes.

"Are you trying to get my attention or do you think my face is hot?"

She jerked back, her heart rate skyrocketing in surprise. "I—I thought you were asleep."

His thick lashes lifted to a sexy half-mast, and he glanced at her. "I was thinking."

"Something good, I hope." She bit her tongue. If she'd chosen that reply from a compiled list of The Ten Most Inane Things To Blurt she couldn't have done worse.

"I was thinking about you." He didn't smile, merely observed her. No doubt his observation included the reddening of her face.

She sat, frozen, wishing she *had* that list of the ten most inane things to blurt, since they had to be better than any response she was coming up with. Apparently her blush was answer enough, because he grinned. "You never knew I thought about you?"

She shook her head.

"I do." He squeezed her wrist. "I didn't mean to take your feelings for granted. I'm sorry."

She tingled where he touched her. Then she began to tingle all over. Very carefully she removed her arm from his fingers. Contact with the man didn't help her mental processes. She rubbed the place where his hand had been and lifted her chin, preparing to tell him his apology was accepted, that she forgave him for his insensitivity. When she opened her mouth nothing came out except a little squawk. She swallowed.

"Are you angry with me?"

She shook her head.

"Good." He closed his eyes. "That's a load off my mind."

She stared at him so long her eyes began to feel prickly. "What are you going to do about the Yum-Yum account?" She realized with horror she'd asked that question out loud.

He didn't respond, just lay there, those sinful lashes curling outward across high, handsome cheekbones.

Had he actually fallen asleep this time? She doubted it, but decided he'd speak when it suited him.

After another few moments, she faced the fact that gazing at him was not the most productive way to spend her time—especially if she planned to stick to her guns about not helping him perpetrate the fraud against Mr. Rufus.

Her thoughts drifted to the few times she'd spoken with the venerable gentleman over the phone. He was always so good-natured and—well, sweet was the only word she could think of that fit.

Hugo Rufus's Yum-Yum Baby Foods had been around since the fifties. He'd been relying on the same advertisements for years. They'd grown stagnant, dated, not changing with the times. Izzy recalled what Mr. Parish had said only a few moments ago. *"He needs me."* She'd let his assertion slip by, barely registering. At the time, she'd been too flummoxed by his nearness to think clearly. She chewed the inside of her cheek, recalling his assertion. *He needs me.*

Izzy wondered if dear Mr. Rufus's fortunes might be in jeopardy? If his private island was mortgaged to the hilt? She turned worriedly toward the window, seeing nothing of the celestial tableau outside. Was Mr. Rufus's advertising search a last-ditch effort to save the stodgy company from going under?

Today's crop of hep-short-attention-span-tell-me-quick-and-loud-or-forget-it Generation-Xer parents needed to get snagged into hearing about Yum-Yum, or the company could die.

She glanced at her boss. He lay there like some sleeping Norse god with really great lips. Her gaze trailed over him, refusing her demands to look out the window.

She'd seen her boss's preliminary ideas for the Yum-Yum campaign, heard the jingle he would have proposed. Patterned for an MTV generation of young parents, what she'd seen was catchy and eye-grabbing. He'd even managed to talk one of today's fastest rising rock groups into being featured in the promotion. The concept was outrageous yet darling—every member of the group happened to be the father of a baby under the age of one. The infants would also be featured. From what Izzy knew of the concept, if that ad campaign didn't sell Yum-Yum Baby Food, nothing on this earth would.

Torn, she glanced at her boss again. If she let herself be totally honest, Gabriel Parish very well could be Yum-Yum's last chance. What if the company went belly up? Thousands of jobs could be lost. Could she forgive herself if she didn't help? Even if it required a tiny lie? She winced. Okay, a pretty big lie?

Why did she suddenly have to believe, with pulse-pounding certainty, that Hugo Rufus *needed* Gabriel Parish—married or not! Little lies, big lies, whatever it took. He needed what Gabriel Parish could give him as urgently as Dawn Day had needed dental help.

With no desire to examine her decision for potential flaws in logic, she placed her hand on her boss's wrist. Realizing what she'd done, she snatched it away. "I—I'll do it, sir."

One corner of his mouth twitched briefly. "I know, Peabody."

He never even opened his eyes.

Izzy's idea of shopping for clothes was to go into a discount store where harried employees hardly had time to point out the dressing rooms, let alone turn the purchase of a shorts outfit into a catered affair.

Of course Izzy had never been to *Tant Mieux,* an exclusive boutique in downtown Miami. Perched awkwardly on a costly Louis XIV chair, she was offered all manner of delectable finger food, as emaciated models breezed by in designer ensembles. Izzy wasn't surprised to see the models flapping long, fake eyelashes at Mr. Parish, while smiling suggestively with collagen-pumped lips.

Neither was she surprised that the gaunt nymphs treated her as though she were a smudge on the brocade upholstery. Something to wrinkle one's nose at, then quickly turn away. Clearly her gray, knee-length suit and gum-soled walking shoes were not on the cutting edge of haute couture.

"Yes," Mr. Parish said, drawing Izzy's attention. "We'll take that one, too."

She glanced at the model posing before her boss. The vixen's expression was so come-hither that Izzy didn't know whether Mr. Parish had purchased the model or the mauve shorts set with matching platform sandals, feathered beanie and color-coordinated polo mallet.

"I hope out back they're not dyeing a horse to match that outfit," she mumbled. For the past two hours she'd sat quietly as her boss made selection after selection. But this purple job was too much! She couldn't be silent any longer.

Mr. Parish glanced her way, hiking a brow. "You have a problem with it?"

"To *which?* A mauve horse or the outfit?"

He leaned her way. "With your brown eyes, you'll look lovely in mauve," he assured with a grin.

Taken off guard by the mention of her eye color, she murmured, "I—I didn't know you ever noticed the color of my eyes."

"I checked in the limo on the way over." He glanced away, toward the next model swaying toward him.

"You didn't have to go to all that bother, sir, I

could have *memoed* you on it.'' Izzy knew she had no right to feel affronted, but she did. After working for him three whole years, he'd only noticed her eyes because he'd made a point to on the way over!

He glanced at her. ''Should I memo you on the color of mine? It's something my *wife* should know about me.''

She swallowed several times. She would never be able to forget those eyes, no matter how she might try. ''No, sir. I—I'll catch a look later.''

He faced her fully, and leaned so close that she could have kissed him with hardly more than a pursing of her lips. ''No time like the present. What do you see?''

Her body reacted violently to his soft question. She felt herself going hot and cold, and blood pounded in her temples. She fought the urge to tip her head forward just enough—just enough...

Fighting the impulse with all her might, she sank back in the seat, praying she looked more composed than she felt. ''Green...I'd say...green.'' Her voice sounded breathless and husky. ''I'll jot it down so I won't forget.'' She made herself look at the mauve-clad model, wiggling toward the exit. ''On the subject of that last outfit, I don't want the hat or the shoes—or the mallet.''

''Loosen up, Peabody.'' He winked, still much too close for her peace of mind. ''You might like it.''

She frowned, fighting the erotic effect of his suggestion. ''My idea of loosening up does *not* include breaking an ankle in those shoes. And I don't think the birdies gave those feathers voluntarily!'' She paused, then added, ''I'm rethinking the mallet.''

He chuckled, taking her veiled threat as a joke.

"You're tired." Turning to the hovering proprietress, he said, "That will be enough. Have everything sent to my hotel this evening."

Izzy was mortified. Though every item of clothing he'd purchased was hugely expensive, many were more suited for a mistress than a wife. At least not a wife about to meet the conservative Mr. Hugo Rufus.

Izzy knew she didn't have a chance at winning an argument with her boss, so she decided to use a little trickery of her own. "Uh, Mr. Parish?"

He turned, his expression one of a man satisfied with the business of the day.

"I think I should stay a while. I'm sure a few things will need alterations."

"Of course." He stood, checking his watch. "Forgive me, Peabody. They are your clothes, after all. You should feel comfortable in them."

She gritted her teeth. *And I'll have tons and tons of places to wear them, too!* she threw back mentally. *I go to so many coronations and White House garden parties!*

"I need to get some work done. Take your time. I'll send the driver back to wait."

"Thank you." She hoped her anxiety over what she planned to do didn't show in her voice.

Once he was gone, she counted to ten, working up her courage to face the shop owner. With hands clasped nervously, she spun around. "I'm going to have to make some changes in Mr. Parish's selections."

The proprietress remained poised, with hardly a flicker of an eyelash to show either surprise or dismay. No doubt many husbands preferred to dwell in their own misguided fantasy that their wives adored their taste. Not that Gabriel Parish wasn't discriminating. But he was a man—a bachelor. And hardly conservative! If they were taking an extended vacation on a yacht with Jack Nicholson and other glittery Hollywood types, the choices would have been appropriate. But *not* for a visit to conventional, family-oriented Mr. Rufus.

"Shall we begin, Miss?" the unruffled shop owner inquired.

Izzy struggled to keep her gaze from wavering in embarrassment. It was evident the woman recognized that Izzy wasn't Mr. Parish's wife. No doubt the fact that Izzy called him "Mr. Parish" was a big hint.

This was an awful moment—one of many Izzy knew she'd have to endure now that she'd promised to go through with this farce. She hoped she hadn't done a very stupid thing—that her foolish desire to be near her boss hadn't run roughshod over her sensible need to leave him—rationalizing a reason for staying.

Riddled with guilt and self-doubt, she forced a smile. "Let's start with that purple polo and poultry outfit."

The flight to Tranquillity Island was scheduled for tomorrow morning. Izzy was exhausted from the long, trying day. She hadn't finished making wardrobe changes and fittings at *Tant Mieux* until nearly eight. Seamstresses had stayed late, a clear indication that the bill had been substantial enough for special considerations.

Izzy brought most of the selections back with her, but the things that needed a bit more altering arrived at nine-thirty.

She took a shower before remembering the night-gowns were lost somewhere in the mountain of boxes and sacks piled around her room. The hotel's white terry robe hanging in her closet caught her eye, saving her from having to dig in all that stuff, wrapped in a bedsheet.

Wearing the robe and matching slippers, she began to towel-dry her hair. A knock at the door brought her head up, then she remembered. Mr. Parish sent a hotel employee out to purchase suitcases for her. No doubt they had arrived. Wrapping the towel around her hair, she peered through the peephole. Unable to see anybody, she cracked the door as far as the se-curity latch would allow. "Hello? Who's there?"

The knock boomed again, this time from behind her. She spun, startled. The sound came from the door that adjoined her room with Mr. Parish's.

"Peabody?"

"Yes, sir?" She wondered what he might want her to do at this hour. She wasn't exactly dressed for dic-tation.

"I've ordered some food. I thought you might be hungry."

Stunned, she sank against the door. It clicked shut. "Food?"

"Peabody, I can't hear you. Let me in."

"Oh—uh…" Accustomed to doing as he bid, she scurried to the door and threw it wide.

He stood there grinning, looking marvelous in beige slacks and a short-sleeved knit shirt, the same bright hue as his eyes. When he scanned her, his grin skewed wryly. "Bad timing?"

At first she didn't register what he meant. Then she remembered she wore nothing but a robe. With suddenly restless fingers she touched her towel turban. "I—I just…" She motioned loosely toward the bathroom.

"I gathered that." He indicated a dining table, set with two covered dishes and a big carafe. "Come. Eat while it's warm."

She peered down at herself. The big robe swallowed her from her chin to the top of her terry scuffs. She certainly wouldn't show any skin he hadn't seen before—and precious little of that. Deciding she could use some food, she stepped into his room.

"It was nice of you to think of me, Mr. Parish." Usually on business jaunts he had dinner engagements with clients. On most of those occasions she went along, took notes, rummaged through files in his briefcase, whatever he needed to make the meeting go smoothly. After dinner, she went to her room and read herself to sleep. *Never* had he ordered room service for them to share.

"You're doing me a favor, Peabody." He pulled out her chair and she took a seat at the glass-topped table. "The least I can do is feed you." He smiled, and she hurriedly turned to gaze out the window. His smiles were too disturbing to experience while wearing nothing but a robe.

She noted with some irritation that her lack of proper attire didn't unsettle him in the slightest. Of course, being a worldly bachelor, seeing half-dressed women was no big event to him.

She concentrated on the view outside the picture window. From their room on the twentieth floor, she scanned Miami's meandering coast, lights adorning the shoreline like a brilliant crown. Farther out, on the dark water, scattered twinkling lights marked oceangoing vessels as they crept across the sleeping sea.

A sound caught her attention and she turned back. Her boss seated himself on the far side of the table—which wasn't far enough. She crossed her legs, her foot skimming his shin. Her slipper fell off.

"Oh…"

"What?" He glanced up from placing his napkin in his lap.

She shook her head, feeling her cheeks heat up. "My slipper—it…"

He looked down. The white scuff was clearly visible beside his brown loafer. "I'll get it." He bent, ducking beneath the table.

"That's not necessary, Mr. Pa—"

He took her ankle into his hand, cutting off her breath. As he lifted her foot, her robe skimmed off her knee, revealing a show of leg. She could see all this through the glass. And because it was glass, there was no stopping the light from passing right through. Mr. Parish had a good clear view, too. Izzy cursed the table for not being made of thick oak.

He remained bent there holding her ankle for a fraction of a second longer before slipping the scuff onto her foot. Did Izzy sense a momentary hesitation, or was it merely a hallucination brought on by the woozy feeling his touch generated in her brain? She had to admit, she wasn't feeling up to her usual, alert self.

He let her go and ducked back out. Brushing a fallen lock of hair off his brow, he grinned. "Cinderella, I'm happy to report the slipper fits."

She dragged her feet beneath her seat and adjusted her robe over her knees. "Actually it's a little big."

He removed the cover from both their meals and gave her a cynical look. "That's my Peabody. Ever the hard-nosed realist. Not a touch of romance in her soul."

She stared at her plate, deciding a close inspection of her cheese soufflé was better than giving him the chance to see the pain and longing in her eyes. Her ankle sizzled unmercifully from the caress of his fingers.

Hard-nosed realist, ha! He couldn't be more wrong. She was *without a doubt* the biggest, stupidest romantic fool who had ever lost her slipper—and her heart—to a man. If that weren't so agonizingly true, she would *not* be on her way to a private island paradise, pretending to be his wife!

His wife.

She had a quick, disturbing revelation. Not until this moment did the true scope of that status hit her. As his wife, she would be expected to spend a certain amount of time alone with him—in a room much like this one.

Panic racing through her, she peered at him. The fact that he was watching her shook her badly, and she could only stare.

An easy smile played at the corners of his mouth. "Don't look so worried, Peabody." He reached across the table, his hand closed as though he held something. "You'll like being Mrs. Parish." With a sexy wink, he slipped a golden wedding band onto her finger.

CHAPTER THREE

THE next morning at eight o'clock, Izzy found herself being handed onto a small, sleek jet by one of two pleasant-looking men in black uniforms and pilots' caps. When she and her boss entered the cabin, Izzy was struck by the exquisitely appointed white leather interior and plush carpeting. The seats were as big and cushy as armchairs, and were separated by small tables, making each grouping an intimate setting for two. There were three such seating areas on either side of the aisle. Two couples were already on board, seated across the aisle from each other in the forward table groupings.

Izzy tried not to show stunned surprise when her boss's hand went to her waist in a display of husbandly affection.

The fraud had begun in earnest.

"Did I tell you how nice you look today?" Mr. Parish whispered.

She went stock-still and stared. "No." His smile was warm and believably loving. If Izzy didn't know better, she would have been convinced her boss was truly devoted to her. *Ha!*

"Then you should be told. You look lovely—darling," he reaffirmed, this time louder.

She lifted her chin and forced a smile. He might as well be complimenting himself. He picked out the dress! She had to admit, the sleeveless frock was beautiful, fashioned out of sand-colored faille and splashed with tropical blossoms and ferns. With its above-the-knee, sarong-wrap skirt, it offered an occasional flash of thigh. Coupled with ankle-strap sandals with high, wedged heels, Izzy didn't think she looked much like an executive assistant. At least not one who could actually type and take dictation.

"Why, thank you—lovikuns." The ridiculous pet name just popped out. Miffed about his manipulations to get her involved in this hoax, she couldn't keep her feelings completely buried. "You know I *live* for your approval." She fluttered her lashes, noting how his forehead wrinkled ever so slightly, though he maintained his devoted-spouse expression.

He coaxed her down the aisle. With the touch of his hand scorching her waist, he bent to whisper, "Lovikuns?" Her ear tickled with the brush of his lips. "Don't overdo it, Peabody."

He took her hand to help her up to the raised seating area. She was surprised when he touched the chair's arm and it swiveled out for easy access. Once again, she kept her surprise to herself. Mr. Parish didn't seem inclined to buy his own plane, at least not yet, so she wasn't accustomed to such unexpected frills. Clearly Mr. Hugo Rufus had a lot to lose if he couldn't find a way to make Yum-Yum a household word again. She wondered how much longer the sweet old man could hold onto his fancy plane.

Once Izzy was settled, Mr. Parish slid into the chair on the other side of the small, marble-top table they shared. Gathering her hand into his, he lifted her fingertips to his lips and brushed them with a kiss. "I think of this trip as a second honeymoon, darling." His eyes held such tenderness she had an urge to turn around to see who he was talking to, but at the last second she remembered her role.

And he said not to overdo it?

"My very thoughts." Her smile was more like a smirk, since she faced away from the other guests. Withdrawing her fingers, she dropped her hand to the table. "But, don't you think we should meet these nice people—lambie-pie?"

His lips twitched wryly at her smart-aleck endearment, but he was hardly in a position to reprimand her, and she knew it. "Of course, darling." Placing a hand over the one she had removed from his, he swiveled to better see those in front of them. He squeezed her fingers. Not enough to give her pain, just reinforce his warning that she not overplay her hand.

Without giving him the satisfaction of a glance, she swung her chair toward the aisle, too, trying not to look too disconcerted. Mr. Parish had touched her more in the past ten minutes than in the entire three years since she'd started working for him. The lingering contact was doing erratic things to her breathing.

Izzy noticed that the other two couples had turned their chairs outward, also. She took a quick survey of Mr. Parish's rivals for the Yum-Yum account. A middle-aged couple sat across the aisle and forward in the cabin. They both wore navy-blue suits and thin-lipped smiles, looking like sallow, humorless bookends.

The other couple was seated on the same side of the aisle as Izzy and her boss. They appeared to be around Mr. Parish's age, tanned and trendy, the kind of moneyed couple you might see at a swanky Club

Med. The blonde with a casual, windswept coif looked as if she might have a tendency to be snooty, the way she peered down her nose. Or she might simply have a stiff neck. Izzy decided to give her the benefit of the doubt.

Her husband had the brawny bulk of a football full-back. His hair was white-blond and thinning, his swarthy face too reminiscent of a pit bull to be considered handsome. They both wore California chic summer clothes, and seemed to have a predilection for gold jewelry.

The pit bull leaned forward. "Name's Wirt. Fox McFarland Wirt, and this is the wife, Claudia." He grinned at the pale, stiff-lipped couple across from him, then at Izzy and Mr. Parish. "Call me Foxie."

Claudia smiled, but her smile, like her husband's, lacked warmth. Nobody was kidding anybody. This trip was no pleasure jaunt. A huge account was at stake. The three couples would be hard-pressed to be more than superficially pleasant.

"Good to meet you, Foxie." Mr. Parish smiled at the man, then his wife. "Claudia." It was a good smile, and Izzy saw only friendliness there. She tried to make hers as engaging, but felt she was having little success. "This is my lovely wife...." He paused. When he squeezed her hand, she glanced his way, curious about the delay. It startled her when he took her chin into his fingers and drew her face toward his, brushing her lips with a light but soul-wrenching kiss. Her body went into quivering, melting shock as he angled her face around to press a kiss against her ear. *"What in hell is your first name, Peabody?"* he whispered. Izzy didn't know how he managed to say anything with his tongue and teeth nipping and stroking. The man had more talents than she'd ever imagined.

Every mental circuit in her brain zapped and snapped, with downed wires writhing all over the place. Yet even with her brain gone haywire, she could detect his annoyance. Belatedly the substance of his question succeeded in rerouting to a functioning part of her brain. He wanted to know her first name. Clearing her thumping heart from her throat, she whispered near his ear, *"Izzy."*

He shifted his gaze to clash with hers, his eyes conveying the message that he would never have guessed anything so appalling could possibly be her name. With a pseudo-devoted pat on her cheek and a dazzling smile, he faced the onlookers. His expression was believably apologetic. "Forgive me. She drives me wild. What were we talking about?"

Izzy felt so discombobulated she wanted to scream. He'd *kissed* her, sending every cell in her body into chaos—*right there in front of everybody*—then he'd crossly admitted that he didn't recall her name! No, screaming was not enough! She wanted to…to…she eyed her boss with scorching intent. She wanted to scratch out his…to…to pluck out…those…those…

The tingling pleasure of his kiss continued to flow through her, making her light-headed. She was too intensely aware of him, of his scent, the lingering heat of his lips, his magnetic eyes gazing lovingly at her.

"You were about to introduce your wife," Foxie said.

Izzy blinked, coming out of a stupor his soft stare brought on.

"Oh, yes. Foxie, was it?" Mr. Parish said. "My wife's name is—Isabel."

"Call me Izzy," she cut in, grateful her lips worked, considering they still sizzled. She passed her fake husband an impertinent look, her emotions a roiling mix of anger, hurt and melancholy. "Lambie-pie loves the nickname, Izzy."

His grin turned lopsided at her gibe, and though she saw a flash of reproach in his gaze, she knew the others couldn't have noticed. "And I'm Gabe Parish."

"Ah, right." Foxie snapped beefy fingers. "I've heard good things about you, my man. The young genius of promotion in the Big Apple."

Gabe lifted his gaze from Izzy. "And I about you, Foxie. L.A.'s hottest ad exec."

"California, my man," Foxie amended, with a guffaw. "California's hottest ad exec."

"I stand corrected." Gabe's glance moved across to the bookends in blue. "And you are?"

"We're Mr. and Mrs. Miles. Hedda and Roger Miles. Chicago. The Miles and Unwin Agency." Mr. Miles straightened his tie. His movements held a prim, brittle dignity that did nothing to indicate a desire to strike up a friendship.

"I've heard of your firm. Good solid reputation," Gabe said. He still held Izzy's hand. As he spoke he laced his fingers with hers. She continued to face Mr. and Mrs. Miles with an expression of interest, but it was difficult. Her heart ached because the intimacy of their entwined fingers was a superficial sham.

"And what do we call you?" Foxie's voice boomed in the cabin. "Rog?"

Roger Miles turned close-set eyes on Foxie. With a sniff of his thin nose, he said, "Roger and Hedda."

Foxie's white-blond brows wagged upward as

though he was amused by the man's frigid tone. "You got it, my man. Roger and Hedda it is."

Izzy scanned Mr. and Mrs. Miles. Clearly they weren't planning to disguise their aversion to their competition, at least until in the presence of their host.

The pilot and copilot climbed aboard. As the crew disappeared up front, an attractive brunette, also clad in a black uniform, entered the plane and began to take drink and breakfast orders.

Not long after Gabe ordered two glasses of gourmet water with a twist of lime, Izzy braced herself for takeoff. She'd never enjoyed the experience. Glancing at her disturbing counterfeit husband, then around at his business rivals, she had a sinking sensation that the white-knuckled takeoff would be the least stressful experience she could expect for the next week.

Gabe only half listened to Claudia and Foxie Wirt name-drop about celebrities they buddied around with in Los Angeles. He smiled and nodded when appropriate, but knew half of what the couple said was bull.

His gaze drifted to Roger Miles, who looked like a bean counter in his conventional blue suit, wing tips and slicked-back graying hair. Gabe wasn't fooled by the drab image. Roger Miles's reputation in the advertising business was well-known. The man was sharp and creative and had won a lion's share of prestigious awards.

Though Roger's advertising campaigns followed more traditional precepts than his gifted young contemporaries, they were consistently clever and effective. Not only that, Roger Miles was more in line with Hugo Rufus's age. That bond alone gave him an edge. Not to mention Fox Wirt's reputation as the top ad man on the West Coast. Gabe had no doubt the competition would be stiff.

Movement caught his eye and he glanced toward Izzy. She crossed her legs and her sarong skirt shifted, one edge slipping away to expose a good portion of thigh. He didn't intend to stare, but for some reason he couldn't look away. Peabody's legs had never entered his mind before now. Of course he hadn't seen much of them. Maybe a flash of knee when she sat down to take dictation, but she had never crossed her legs in his presence. She always sat like a little soldier, shoulders back, sensible shoes planted squarely on the floor. For some reason he hadn't thought of Peabody as the leg-crossing type. Or even *having* legs for that matter.

As he scanned the pale flesh from her knee up to where the fabric overlapped, just below her panty line, he noticed the limb was slender, with attractively feminine muscle definition under the skin. He wondered if she exercised. He'd never thought about Peabody exercising. She didn't look like the type who would work up a sweat either physically or emotionally.

"Say, Gabe, my man. Where's your mind?"

Hearing his name, his glance shot to Foxie. "Excuse me?"

The big Californian grinned and cocked his head toward Izzy. "Can't get your mind or your eyes off her for a second?" He made a clucking sound of feigned disapproval. "Old married men like us aren't supposed to be lusting after our wives all the time. Gives marriage a bad name."

Izzy turned toward Gabe, her expression puzzled. She wore her hair up, as usual, but there was something different about the way she'd done it. Wispy strands framed her face giving her a softer look. It wasn't exactly in a bun, either, more of a swirl. He didn't think she had on makeup, but her face was somehow altered, too.

He knew she was irritated with him—especially about the kiss. He'd barely brushed her lips, but to a prim thing like Peabody, even that would be a flagrant breach of propriety. She was doubtless mortified. He didn't blame her, but he'd had no choice. As he scanned her puzzled expression he had to admit she looked rather pretty today. Her indignation added radiance to her eyes and an attractive blush to her cheeks.

Even as uncomfortable as she was about this scheme, Gabe had to give her credit. She was a good sport. With a grin that didn't have to be manufactured, he lifted her fingertips and rubbed them against his jaw. "Forgive my distraction, Foxie. Repeat what you said. I promise you my complete attention."

Gabe felt Peabody go tense the instant her knuckles touched his face, but gamely, she pasted on a smile before facing Foxie.

The blond man rambled on about movie stars he'd gone deep-sea fishing with. Izzy recrossed her legs and the dress fabric slid to cover her thigh. Gabe suddenly became aware that he'd not only lost the thread of the conversation again, but he'd actually been *ogling* Peabody's leg.

Wincing, he snapped his gaze away. *Good Lord, Parish!* he admonished inwardly, *it's been too long since you were with a woman!*

If his straight-laced little fake wife had any inkling of where his mind had been, she would be scandalized!

To Izzy, the fifty-minute flight to Tranquillity Island seemed like a month. By the time the jet was in sight of their destination, she knew as much about Foxie and Claudia Wirt as she cared to know. Her cheeks hurt from forcing a smile, and she felt sure this was only the beginning. With a surge of dismay, Izzy decided she *deserved* aching cheek muscles—at the very least—for her part in this fraud.

The plane circled, lining up to the runway. Talk stopped and the plane's occupants swiveled to gaze out their windows. Izzy noticed that the upper curve of the island was dominated by a volcano, its craggy face rising through white puffs of clouds.

"I hope that's extinct," she murmured, startled to hear her fear voiced aloud.

"It is."

She swiveled to see the flight attendant, retrieving plates and glasses from the tables. Izzy smiled, relieved. "Thanks. My idea of a vacation isn't to be buried under a ton of ash."

"Spoilsport," Gabe kidded.

She glanced his way. Unfortunately for her, the sunlight hit him just right, and his eyes shone like expensive emeralds. Disconcerted, she quickly looked out her window.

From the volcano's summit to its heavily forested foothills, the half-moon-shaped isle boasted a lush palate of greens, impressive in the morning sun, but not as impressive as a certain pair of eyes. Eyes she could still feel on her—laughing at her. She worked at concentrating on the scenery below. Bordering the

island like a pink-and-white fringe lay miles of un-
interrupted beach, caressed by a turquoise ocean that
spread out as far as the eye could see.

The lower curve of the island held the only visible
touch of man. A pale stone mansion towered amid
manicured lawns, meandering granite walkways and
elaborate, kaleidoscopic gardens.

"It's like stepping into another century," Izzy murmured.

"Except for the runway." Gabe's comment drew
her reluctant gaze. "Unless it's some ancient alien
landing strip."

His lips tipped up at the corners, his big hand
squeezing hers with teasing familiarity. Her heart
jolted. Gabe Parish had no idea how unkind he was
being to her with his bogus loving touches and
glances. In order to keep her composure, at least superficially, she peered out the window.

Off to the left of the palace grounds, beyond a thick
border of trees, lay a ribbon of black—doubtless, the
airstrip they were headed for. Izzy caught sight of
teensy moving objects on the tarmac's edge.

People!

The jet touched down and skimmed along the runway, taxiing toward the gathering. Izzy watched the
assemblage as the plane slowed to a stop. At first she
couldn't quite believe what she saw. Several members
of the small group were playing instruments. In front
of the others was a wiry gentleman with a snow-white
crop of hair, waving. She wondered if this friendly
elf of a man was their host, Hugo Rufus.

Watching him wave broadly with both hands tickled her and she waved back, though she knew they
were too far away for him to see. As the plane slowed

to a stop, she studied him. His chin was pointy, his ears jutted out and he had a smile like one of those "happy face" stickers, giving him even more the look of a merry elf. His bright orange T-shirt read, Before They Made Me, They Broke The Mold!

Izzy stifled a giggle. If the man waving them in was Hugo Rufus, he was about as far away from a stuffed shirt as a company CEO could get. She liked him already.

"Is that shirt just witty, or a warning?" Gabe said, more to himself than to anyone.

Izzy glanced his way. He squinted out the window, apparently not sure how to take their host. She supposed Gabe hadn't attended many business gatherings that called for neon T-shirts sporting wacky slogans.

Her grandmother on her mother's side, Dora McBeal, had been a professional dancer on Broadway, decades ago. Even now, the sprightly woman taught ballroom dancing, mainly to senior citizens groups. When she did, she wore jeans and T-shirts, most of them with funny sayings like Hugo's. Granny Dorie lived every day to the fullest, laughed a lot and never took anything too seriously.

After working for Gabe, watching him drive himself, Izzy had begun to see how wise her grandmother's happy-go-lucky philosophy was. Granny Dorie had been a driven woman in her earlier years, determined to be a success on Broadway. She'd begun her family rather late, after discovering stardom wasn't all it was cracked up to be. Izzy sensed Hugo had learned the same lesson somewhere along the line—to take time to enjoy life, rather than barrel through it with blinders on.

Stirring sounds around her brought her back to the

present. She noticed Gabe watching her. He lifted a hand, a silent offer to help her from her seat. Straightening her shoulders, she got into character. "Thank you—*sweetums*." She eyed him narrowly, fine-tuning her smile. "I can't wait to meet Mr. Rufus." That, at least, wasn't a lie.

Foxie's laugh boomed. "Look at that boob! And I was worried about getting my presentation classy enough."

Claudia tittered. "He looks so silly."

Izzy gritted her teeth. Of all the pompous, arrogant, narrow-minded things to say! Her opinion of the Wirts dive-bombed.

"I think he's *cute*." Irritated, she turned toward Gabe and lifted her chin in wordless challenge. After all, considering what she was doing for him, he could at least pretend to agree with her. "Don't you think Mr. Rufus is cute, sweetie?" She didn't know why she had to defend the elderly man, but she did. Maybe it was for all senior citizens, like Granny Dorie, who chose not to vegetate, but opted to live fully and never lose their sense of humor.

Izzy noticed a vague lift of Gabe's brows, the only outward indication that he was startled by her thin-lipped assertion. Obviously he hadn't expected passion from his mild-mannered Peabody. An easy grin played across his lips. Izzy found herself pondering if he was aware of the irresistible picture he made when he smiled. *He knew, the crafty hunk!*

Pushing up from his seat, Gabe tugged her to stand. "A man would be a fool to contradict his wife—on the threshold of his second honeymoon." He stepped down into the aisle, then encircled her waist with his hands, lifting her to the lower level. As the flight attendant opened the door, Gabe slid a hand upward along her back, then drew her beneath his arm. Izzy felt light-headed, both by the sensuality of his remark and his possessive touch. No wonder women had actual fistfights over the man. *He was good!*

Izzy registered the thrilling trail his fingers had taken along her back as they stepped off the plane. She continued to experience the tingling sensation while he led her toward Hugo Rufus and his four-piece band.

Hugo hurried forward to greet them, his arms outstretched. A rosy, soft little woman flitted along beside him wearing a nostalgic tea dress of pale pink. They carried what looked like dozens of colorful Hawaiian leis. The musicians, in white Bermuda shorts and color-happy shirts, struck up a rousing welcome.

Hugo took his companion's hand as they approached, and she blushed like a schoolgirl. Clearly she was Hugo's wife, and loved the man fiercely and with great pride. Izzy watched the woman gaze at Hugo, and experienced a pang of envy. Gabe's fingers on her shoulder began to tap out the beat of the music, and she gulped around a harsh lump in her throat. If only his touch meant what it appeared to mean—if only Gabe Parish really...

She couldn't bring herself to think such a hopeless thing.

The tune ended as Hugo and his wife reached the group. "Welcome, welcome! I'm your host, and this lovely lady is my wife, Clara." Hugo beamed. "I know we're a long way from Hawaii, but one of my cooks loves to make Hawaiian leis, so I indulge her." He and his wife moved to opposite ends of the group of visitors and began slipping leis over each person's head. "I think offering leis to new arrivals is an enchanting custom, don't you?"

Izzy received two leis from Clara. As the shorter woman placed the flowered adornments around Izzy's neck, she couldn't help but be captivated by the quiet contentment in Clara's eyes. It was obvious the woman loved Hugo dearly, even when it was becoming apparent that their host had a charming eccentricity or two. Izzy hoped one day she would find someone who would love her that strongly. No questions asked, no compromises required. Just pure, wholehearted love.

Gabe removed his arm from around her so he could bend low enough for Clara to drop three leis over his head. Izzy caught a glimpse of the Mileses and could tell their polite smiles were pained. She doubted that they considered flowers around the neck proper business attire.

When the leis were all handed out, Hugo stepped back to admire his guests. "Truly a photographer's dream. You all look splendid!" He grinned with delight. "Oh, but I forget my manners." Stepping up to Roger, he reached out to grasp his hand. "Was the flight rough?" Hugo pumped Roger's arm with both of his. "You and Mrs. Miles look a little gray."

"No." Roger's brow was pinched. "It was quite smooth. Thank you."

"Are you absolutely sure?" Hugo looked concerned. "Then it's flying that disagrees with you. I know how it can be for some people. Makes me queasy, too."

"I'm fine." Roger pulled his hand free. "Thank you."

Hugo appeared unconvinced, but moved to the

gaunt woman in blue linen. "Hedda, is it?" Izzy
watched the woman nod stiffly and gingerly accept
her host's hand. "And you, my dear? You're feeling
a touch of mal de mer, I can tell. Or should I say mal
de *air?*" He chortled. "No matter. A few days in this
bracing air and sunshine will fix you right up."

Hedda Miles expression exhibited a trace of alarm,
as though the idea of being out in the sun frightened
her.

"No—no," she was insisting, "I'm quite fit, really."

"Splendid! Splendid," Hugo said. "Nevertheless,
I'll have some ginger ale sent to your room as soon
as we get back."

Izzy peeked at Gabe. Laughter flickered in his eyes
and lurked at the corners of his mouth as Mrs. Miles
endured Hugo's spirited handshake. Clearly the
woman felt physical contact was good only for trans-
porting disease germs from one person to another.
Poor inhibited, neurotic Hedda.

Izzy knew Gabe wouldn't have a problem with
Hugo's extravagant welcome, even if the man threw
his arms around Gabe in a hearty bear hug. One thing
she'd learned about her boss in the past hour was that
he had no reluctance about touching. It was a skill he
could use with a vengeance.

Hugo moved on to big blond Foxie and his perfectly coiffed wife. Taking each hand in turn, he
pumped with abandon, making effusive, friendly conversation. He seemed to mean every word; Izzy
couldn't detect a hint of duplicity in his expression
or manner. He was like a hyperactive puppy who
loved everybody and assumed they would love him

right back. She grew crazier about their host by the minute.

When he reached Izzy, he took her hand in his. His grip was firm and warm, but not cloying. "Ah, my dear Mrs. Parish. Welcome!" He scanned her face. With the reminder of the lie, she knew she was blushing but she couldn't help it. "I needn't ask how you're feeling. You have the flush of health in your cheeks." He held her hand in both of his for a moment longer, then released her. "What shall I call you? I didn't quite hear when you told Clara."

"Izzy."

He laughed, a twittery peal of mirth. "You look exactly like an Izzy, my dear. The very essence of effervescence!"

She grinned at his comical description. He was even enthusiastic about her name. What a delightful human being. "I love your shirt," she said before realizing she'd spoken aloud. "Er, my grandmother has a collection of T's with funny sayings. My favorite has an old Yugoslavian proverb on it that reads Tell The Truth And Run." Abruptly the irony hit her—she was going to spend the next seven days *lying* to this sweet man. All happiness drained from her in a *whoosh*. She felt deflated, stained.

"I must get that one!" His dark eyes sparkled with pleasure, making her feel worse. "Your grandmother is a woman after my own heart."

She murmured something in response. Hugo's smile didn't dim, so he must not have noticed the rapid about-face of her mood. Gloom hovered around her as Hugo shook Gabe's hand and chatted with him.

"Well, now that we're all acquainted, welcome, all, to my Shangri-la!" Hugo said, snapping her back.

"I'm sure we're going to have a dipsy-doodle of a time." He raised his arms and beckoned. "Enough blathering in the heat. Let's go inside where you can refresh yourselves and get settled before lunch is served."

Izzy felt Gabe's arm settle around her shoulders as they were led to a row of bright yellow golf carts for the ride to the mansion. Gabe drove their cart in silence. Weighed down by guilt, Izzy absently looked around. She noticed Foxie had taken the lead with his cart. He and his wife were laughing about something. She hoped to goodness they weren't making fun of Hugo. If they were, they didn't deserve the account.

Gabe glanced at her and then back at the meandering stone lane they rode over. "So you're the essence of effervescence, Peabody?" A chuckle rumbled in his chest. "We've been here fifteen minutes and you're already his favorite spouse."

She didn't look at him. "He just likes my name." *And I'm not a spouse!* she shot back mentally.

"Whatever. He's nuts about you…I can tell."

She set her jaw and stared straight ahead. She was nuts about Hugo, too. She'd hated the scheme when it had only been in the planning stage, but now that they were knee-deep in it, the *reality* was a hundred times worse.

Another chuckle drew her attention and she peered his way. "What?"

"I don't know what I expected but that cross between Pollyanna and Jiminy Cricket wasn't it."

"Me, neither." Her tone conveyed her dejection. She glanced away. They traveled through a cool, wooded patch, heavy with musky, earthy scents. Any other time Izzy would have been thrilled with the quiet beauty of the wood. "I like Hugo, and I don't like what we're doing to him."

"We're not doing anything to him, Peabody."

She heard the exasperation in his tone and frowned. "You have a real flair for rationalizing, sir."

He cast her a brief glance. A shadow of annoyance skittered over his features. "Keep your voice down." For a few heartbeats he said nothing, but a muscle flicking in his jaw left little question about his frame of mind. "There's nothing to be done about it, so let's make the best of the situation."

She stared straight ahead, surprised at his uncharacteristic show of temper. Was he beginning to feel bad about duping the old man, too, or did he simply wish that the lovely Dawn Day was here beside him instead of her?

"Smile, Peabody," he whispered. "Snuggle up next to me." He lifted an arm to pull her close. "Remember, we're supposed to be in love. Hugo and his wife aren't far behind us." He drew her against him, rubbing her arm fondly, up and down, up and down.

His scent mingled nicely with the earthy smells of the shady lane. His masculine torso felt so right. She had a foolish urge to grab him and hold on forever. How simple it would be to take him in her arms, close her eyes and put aside the ugly fact that this was all a sham. In a safeguarding move, she wadded her hands in her lap to keep from doing anything reckless.

"Peabody," he whispered against her hair, "I think you should put your hand on my thigh."

Izzy bit her lip until it throbbed.

CHAPTER FOUR

SHE glared at him, shocked. "Have you lost your mind?"

Gabe's low laugh vibrated through her shoulder, where her body touched his. "This isn't sexual harassment, Peabody," he said. "You're supposed to be my wife."

"I don't care. I will not *fondle* your thigh!"

"I didn't say fondle." He lifted his arm from around her and lay a hand on her skirt, just above her knee. He squeezed slightly. "Does that compromise either of us?"

Her breath caught, her speech processes momentarily disabled. He replaced his arm around her, stroking and caressing her shoulder, once again.

"Well?" he prompted into her hair.

Speechless, she stared straight ahead, wishing the heat of his hand didn't linger on her thigh.

"Rufus and his wife can't see where my hands are unless they have X-ray vision."

Izzy sensed Gabe turn her way but didn't meet his eyes. "Peabody, you're a prude."

"Call me whatever name you please, sir." She peered at him. "But I'm the only wife you brought— for better or for worse." Izzy wasn't a prude at all. She simply didn't want to play touchy-feely games with a man who—well, who was playing a game!

"What if we have to kiss. Are you going to slap me?"

"We've already kissed, sir!" She looked away, suddenly all hot and cold and breathless.

"That?" She felt his low chuckle. "Peabody that was about as close to a kiss as a dripping faucet is to Niagara Falls." He shook his head, the movement drawing her troubled stare. When their glances met, he smiled crookedly. "If we *have* to kiss, try not to punch me. Okay?"

She glowered at him. "Don't kiss me and we won't have to worry about it."

His teasing smirk grew into a full-fledged grin. "Just don't punch me, Peabody."

She didn't like his cheerful expression. It was evident that her boss didn't take her warning seriously. Even worse, he seemed to be implying that a kiss was on their horizon. Panic darted through her, making her light-headed. If what they'd shared on the plane hadn't been a kiss—well, she didn't know what to think.

One thing she was sure of, though, Gabe wouldn't have to worry about being slapped if he *really* kissed her. She would collapse at his feet in a dead faint. She'd let him worry about how to explain that!

"Nice little place." Gabe's quiet comment drew her from her brooding thoughts.

Izzy realized they'd reached the edge of the shady woods. Following his gaze, she stared in awe. Before her, beyond a green, upwardly sloping lawn and a Shangri-la of flower gardens, the Rufus mansion glowed in the sunlight.

Built of light-colored stone, the structure loomed there, a symmetrical work of art, swathed in columns, friezes and cornices—a romanticized image of Southern plantation homes of a century ago. Its colonnaded porch was two stories tall, the second floor ringed with balconies of ornamental ironwork. All windows soared from floor to ceiling, combining with the other dramatic proportions to create a vision of grandeur. Yet, nestled in such fairyland surroundings, the stately residence seemed remarkably open and inviting.

"It's like stepping into *Gone With the Wind*," Izzy murmured.

"Glad you came, now?"

Her buoyant mood fizzled. "You must think I'm very shallow to believe that a fancy house would make all the difference." What was worse, Izzy didn't like the idea that Hugo might lose all this if he didn't find the perfect advertising campaign. "Actually, now that I've seen it, I feel even more terrible."

He laughed. "You'd better stick a smile back on your face, Peabody, or I might kiss you."

She turned on him. "Is that a threat?"

His smile grew boyishly teasing. "Absolutely."

After Gabe's taunting, Izzy lost track of everything but the memory of those roguishly tempting lips grinning at her. She vaguely noticed the interior of the manor, registering its richness even in her stupor. Dully she recalled climbing the spiral staircase, her corkscrewed journey doing little to alleviate her giddiness. She didn't know what to think, or how to respond to his soft needling.

Her emotions warred. She didn't want Gabe to kiss her, and he knew it. So he decided to taunt her with warnings of doing just that if she didn't keep up their pretense. Yet another side of her sobbed, deep inside her soul, craving the touch of his lips against hers—

not as a form of coercion or in a mockery of affection. But in true, heartfelt...

"Earth to Peabody?"

Gabe's statement, plus his hand coming down on her shoulder, brought her back to reality. She blinked. They were alone together—in a bedroom. She stared at him in question.

"Are you okay?" he asked. "You seemed to be a thousand miles away."

She felt stupid. Shrugging out from beneath his hand, she nodded. "I'm fine." With feigned nonchalance, she looked around. "Pretty room." That wasn't quite the word for it. Palatial was closer.

With its lofty ceiling and tall windows, the chamber had an open, airy feel. The mahogany furniture was a pleasing mix of English and American styles, magnificent against the background of neutral colors.

A canopy bedstead dominated, hung with hand worked lace and dressed with an embroidered spread. Izzy could only gaze in awe. The bed was a fine antique, far smaller than the king-size beds available today. With another quick, distraught glance around, she faced the harsh fact that there wasn't another piece of furniture in there that could sleep a grown person. Not even the Sheraton fancy chairs, pulled together, would allow a person older than three a comfortable berth.

She spied two other doors. Hope billowing in her breast, she hurried to the nearest and flung it wide. A closet. Her momentary dejection was quickly replaced by new, determined anticipation as she hurried to the other door. Pulling it open, she stared into a bathroom. It was a good size, but hardly anything in there would make a good bed. The antique bathtub was the only prospect. She could try to sleep in it, but it would be far from comfortable. She couldn't even imagine a man as tall and broad as Gabe crumpled in it. He'd have to wad himself up like an old sock.

"Does it pass inspection?" the old sock asked from close behind her.

She jerked around, thumping a hand to her chest. "You startled me!"

He shrugged, sliding his hands into his slacks pockets. "Remember, me?" He winked. "I'm the roommate."

How could she forget? "Oh—right..."

Turning away, she noticed the wall opposite the bed. There were at least thirty pictures grouped above a tall dresser. All held photos of babies or toddlers, framed in silver. She walked over to scan the display. "My goodness." She touched a frame that appeared slightly crooked and straightened it. "These can't be Hugo and Clara's children."

She heard Gabe's muffled footsteps as he approached across the Oriental rug. "If they are, my hat's off to the man for his stamina."

"If they are, your hat should be off to Clara."

He came into her line of vision, and she could tell he was looking at her. "Point taken."

She got a whiff of his aftershave, didn't like its melting effect and spun away, heading toward their floor-to-ceiling windows. Pressing the handles, she unlatched the double doors and stepped out onto their balcony. A sea breeze ruffled loose wisps of hair that tickled her cheeks and forehead. She breathed deeply of the tangy salt air, struggling for composure.

Even with the serene beauty of the place, Izzy's mood plunged to new depths. Until she'd spied that bed, she hadn't thought through the reality of her situation. For the next seven days and *nights* she and Gabe must share this bedroom. How many times in her fantasies had she pictured a room like this, of sharing a cozy bed with the gorgeous likes of Gabe Parish? But in her fantasies, his eyes glowed with passion for her. In actuality, Gabe's gaze hardly strayed to "his Peabody" at all—let alone probed the depths of her soul with wordless communications of love.

A knock at the door drew her attention, and she turned. "Knock, knock!" came Hugo's voice as the door swung open. There he stood, carrying their suitcases. "I hope you're pleased with the room," he said brightly, though Izzy could hear a touch of breathlessness in his words.

She was so stunned to see their host burdened down with their cases, she couldn't seem to react.

Gabe recovered first and moved to the door, taking their suitcases from Hugo's hand. "I apologize about the bags. I didn't realize you were shorthanded."

"Not at all, my boy. It gives me pleasure to help." He reached back and drew something from his pocket. When he held it out, Izzy could see it was a flower, its petals a lovely shade of peach. She didn't recognize it, but decided it must be tropical. "This is for you, Izzy." She moved forward to accept, and he bowed. "It's the color of your cheeks. From now on, I shall always think of it as the Izzy flower." With a jaunty salute, he backed out the doorway. "Now you two relax and refresh. Lunch will be in an hour."

An instant later the door closed. Izzy and Gabe were once again alone. Instinctively she sniffed the delicate blossom. Its scent was light and sweet. With the petals still poised at her nose, she eyed Gabe. He watched her with a grin and shook his head. "I think Hugo has a crush on you, Peabody."

She dropped her hand to her side, suddenly very sad. Moving to the balcony door, she leaned against the jamb. Apparently, witnessing her solemn expression had its effect on Gabe, for his grin disappeared. "What's wrong?"

"You can't possibly *not* know."

"I can't not?" The bedroom rumbled with his soft mirth. "I hate deciphering double negatives, Peabody. Why don't you say what's on your mind, straight out."

"That poor, dear man had to bring up the bags himself. He's worse off than I could possibly have imagined."

Gabe pursed his lips. "Oh, that." He ran a hand across his mouth. "That was a—shock."

She sighed, depressed. Hugo's financial difficulty wasn't the only calamity she had to look straight in the eye at the moment. Reluctantly she shifted to scan the tripod table beside the worrisome bed.

"Something else?" he asked.

She jumped at the sound of his voice. Deciding there was no point in putting it off, she forced herself to meet his gaze. "Where are *you* going to sleep?"

His lips opened slightly, the only manifestation of his surprise. A second later his eyes grew openly amused. "Why, with you—darling."

Gabe checked his watch. Dinner was scheduled for eight o'clock and it was nearly that now. Izzy disappeared into their bathroom an hour ago. Even though Gabe wasn't a married man, he was aware that women took a long time to dress. However, he'd never thought of Izzy as falling into that category. He always assumed she came fully assembled—Executive Assistant Model Number Five-five-nine or JVQ or something.

Tonight's dinner wasn't "black-tie" as he'd anticipated. The dress code was "relaxed casual," whatever that might mean to an off-center character like Hugo. Gabe had decided on a gray linen sports coat and cream gabardine trousers—as relaxed and casual an outfit as his twenty-four-hours-a-day-seven-days-a-week corporate wardrobe could manage.

He'd passed the last thirty minutes jotting in a small notebook he kept with him, nipping and tweaking his ideas for his Yum-Yum presentation. Restless, he pushed up from the edge of the bed, where he'd been sitting, and jammed the notebook into his inside breast pocket. He wasn't a man who relaxed well, always needed to have a project going. He supposed some people would think that trait a flaw, but he wouldn't be where he was today if he idled his time away.

With growing impatience, he watched the second hand make another ponderous trip around the face of his watch. Slanting a perturbed squint at the bathroom door, he gave it a couple of raps. "Peabody, are you *making* your dress?"

"I'll be ready in one more second, sir."

He shook his head. "I've heard that before, Peabody, but I never expected to hear it from you."

She didn't answer.

"Surely it doesn't take you this long to get ready every morning. You'd have to get up at four."

No response.

"If you need help fastening something, I can do it."

Nothing.

Gabe eyed the closed portal with the same degree of frustration men have suffered for thousands of years while staring at doors behind which their women primped. He rapped again. "Peabody, are you dead?"

He heard a noise, and noticed the doorknob turning.

When Izzy came out, she scurried by him so quickly he took a half step back in surprise.

"I'm ready."

"The place isn't on fire. There's no need to run."

When she turned, she was already at the door, her hand on the knob. Her expression solemn, her eyes were big and round and reticent. "I thought you wanted to go."

He scanned her, critically. She wore her hair down. It fell in soft curls to a few inches below her shoulders. He'd never realized she had so much hair. Parted on the side, a wave fell forward, half masking one eye. There was something vaguely provocative about that wide, brown eye playing peekaboo from behind a curtain of hair.

She pressed the curl back, but it fell forward again. The half-hidden eye blinked, the involuntary reflex seeming to blend a womanly come-hither proposal with a little girl's game of hide-and-seek. He winced. What a ludicrous thought for a grown man to have.

Deciding he'd better move on in his thinking, he examined her clothing, not recognizing the dress. He corrected himself. Not a dress, exactly. She wore a sleeveless, fitted white vest top and black pants. The pants were wide-legged. They looked like a skirt, except when she walked, which displayed the fact that they were some kind of trousers with an outer, gossamer layer. He quirked a brow. "Why have I never seen that before?"

She visibly swallowed. "You don't like it?"

He couldn't answer no and be honest. "That's not the point, Peabody. What happened to the things *I* picked out?"

Her chin rose the tiniest fraction. "I imagine that rock star, Madonna, has purchased most of them by now."

He recognized the sarcasm and it surprised him. He kept forgetting Peabody had a sharp wit; she used it so rarely. "Are you suggesting I have no taste?"

"No, sir." She sucked in a shuddery breath. The combination of her bravado mixed with her obvious trepidation was oddly endearing. "I'm saying, I didn't think Hugo Rufus would find some of the things you picked out traditional enough—for a wife."

He gave her another long examination, knowing that beneath those loose slacks her knees probably trembled. With a quirk of his lips, he advanced on her and took her elbow. "You could be right, Peabody." When he put his hand over hers on the doorknob, she slipped her fingers from beneath his. The goosey move irked him. He wasn't an ogre, was he? He didn't shout at her or harass her. When had he given her cause to fear him? "Is that why you stayed in the bathroom so long?" he asked, more gently. "You were afraid of what I'd say?"

"No, sir." Her shoulders were back, her cheeks pinker than he could ever recall. "I was just dressing. Whether you expected it of me or not, I take as long to get ready as any *real* woman."

Her gibe brought on a surge of wry amusement. Peabody had spunk. At least she wasn't so intimidated she couldn't properly defend herself. "I stand corrected." With a courtly nod, he opened the door, indicating that she precede him. "Shall we go down to dinner—darling?"

When she didn't immediately move, he nudged her in the small of her back. "Get going, Peabody," he teased. "Don't force me to kiss you."

With a vexed peek at him, she scurried out the door. It was all he could do to hold back a roar of laughter.

Izzy tried to concentrate on her surroundings. Unfortunately she had a difficult time paying attention to anything but the touch of Gabe's hand, cupping her waist, as he guided her down the spiral staircase.

Grasping the rosewood banister for support, she forced her attention to the richness of the manor, with its expanses of beautifully figured mahogany and rosewood furniture, marble, Chinese silks and cut crystal. The guests had spent much of the day touring the place. Clara Rufus led the excursion, giving the mansion's history, room by room, in her soft-spoken way.

Hugo hovered around his guests, asking after their well-being, an amiable combination of medical doctor and head waiter. The more Izzy saw of their host, the more she adored him.

The dining hall lay directly off the spacious foyer. It was a huge, impressive room with a grand bay window that faced the ocean. The small band, ensconced in a corner, played softly as they entered.

Hugo dashed to greet them, wearing a multicolored

shirt and mauve walking shorts. Izzy focused on their host's animated greeting. He was treating them like long lost loved ones. She laughed and chatted with him, hoping that concentrating on his friendly banter would take her mind off Gabe's disturbing touch.

They were seated at a gorgeous Duncan Phyfe table, offering a spectacular view of the ocean, as well as Roger and Hedda Miles, who sat across the table from them. The Chicago couple looked pale and stiff. Izzy smiled but got no response as the band segued into "Havin' A Heat Wave."

Somehow the Latin American flavor of the composition seemed more appropriate to an island hut rather than this opulence. She scanned the room. Tawny beige walls were offset by white Ionic columns and adorned on three walls with paintings by great masters. On the fourth wall, at the far end, another large grouping of silver-framed children twinkled in the muted light of the chandeliers. Izzy promised herself she'd ask Hugo what all those children were to him.

Hugo seated himself. "I hope everybody had a relaxing afternoon." He motioned toward a couple of sarong-clad women, standing in a doorway, and they began to serve. Izzy was relieved to see them. At least the sweet man hadn't had to lay off everyone—yet. "Of course," he was saying, "house tours being what they are, you were all very brave and polite to stay awake."

Izzy smiled at his joke. Once again, he reminded her of her fun-loving Granny Dorie. She couldn't wait for them to meet. In a painful flash, her mood fell, with a troubling realization. Hugo and Granny Dorie could *never* meet. *Don't forget*, she counseled silently, *you're here under false colors.*

"So, Gabe," Hugo said, lifting his fork. "Tell me about yourself. Your family."

Izzy perked up. She'd been with this man practically night and day for the past three years and she knew nothing about him, personally, except that he had an older sister, and his parents had retired to South Carolina.

She watched his face, working to keep her expression one of wifely indulgence—as though she knew all this in every ho-hum detail.

"I'm the black sheep of my family." His grin was wry. "Considering the fact that both my parents and my sister became cardiovascular surgeons, my decision to go into advertising was a great blow." His rich laughter tingled through Izzy. "They refer to me as their son who ran away to join the circus."

"They do?" Izzy bit down on her lip. How could she have said that out loud? "I—I mean, they *do!*" She laughed. The effort was faulty. Luckily, since Hugo and Clara burst out laughing, too, she decided her unease wouldn't be detectable. "Can you imagine?" she added, with more conviction. "Gabe, my own little black sheep."

At least, now, she understood why he was such a workaholic. With a family of overachievers like his, he had no idea there was any other way to live.

Gabe glanced her way and startled her when he brushed a strand of hair behind her ear. "I love the way you never tire of that joke, darling." His smile made her go all quivery. *Heavens, he was smooth.*

Hugo took a bite of his avocado soufflé, so Izzy did, too. She was starving. "Well, my effervescent

Mrs. Parish," he said, "I hope you and Gabe plan to have children."

Izzy's bite of soufflé lodged in a lung. At least that's what it felt like while she choked. After a scary few seconds, she managed to get a breath. With watery eyes, she faced Hugo and smiled feebly.

What was she to say? Making a quick decision, she resolved she could at least be truthful about her intentions in that area. "Yes, I…" She cleared the rusty sound from her throat and took in another gulp of air. "I look forward to having children."

"Oh, that's wonderful," Hugo said. "My sense about people tells me you'll make a wonderful mother."

Izzy smiled shyly. She wanted nothing more in the world. She just didn't have any potential "daddies" in her life. With regret, she forced herself not to look at Gabe, or dwell on foolish dreams. By some miracle, she managed to hold on to her pleasant expression.

Desperate to focus the conversation away from herself, she waved toward the wall of baby pictures. "Speaking of children, who are all these?"

Hugo's grin faltered for an instant, or did it only seem that way? Izzy couldn't be sure. "Why, they're mine, my dear." He raised his water goblet in a toast. "To my family." After everyone joined in and sipped, Hugo said, "Over the years proud parents have sent me hundreds of pictures of children who are growing up happy and healthy on Yum-Yum food. I treasure them all as though they were my own."

Izzy watched his face. He looked as though he truly did. The fact that there were hundreds of photographs scattered throughout the mansion spoke of how much those children meant to him. "How sweet," she murmured.

Foxie said something, drawing Hugo's attention. Izzy scanned the wall of pictures, again, wondering if Hugo had children of his own. Surely he did, a man so full of love—

Gabe squeezed her hand beneath the table, startling the breath from her. He leaned very near and she reacted to his unexpected closeness with equal parts dread and anticipation. "You did a good job with that lie about children." He grinned, as though amazed at her ability for glib subterfuge.

"I wasn't lying," she whispered. "I *want* lots of children."

His mouth skewed into a crooked smirk that made it clear he thought she was putting him on. "Sure. When will you have time for children, working as my assistant?"

"What's all the buzz-buzz-buzzing about?" Hugo cut in. "Gabe? Izzy? Secrets?"

She shot a guilt-ridden look toward the head of the table. "Oh—I'm sorry. Gabe was just…" She had no idea what to say. Lies didn't flow as easily off her tongue as her boss seemed to think.

"We were discussing babies," Gabe said.

The truth? Izzy looked at her counterfeit husband, confused.

His dazzling smile caused a hot ache of longing in her breast. "She was reminding me she wants a large family."

"Reminding" isn't quite the right word, she charged mentally. *Informing is more like it. As if he cared!*

Gabe slipped his hand up beneath Izzy's hair and began to massage her nape. As his fingers caressed and stroked, her pulse went haywire.

Hugo's eyes twinkled with expectation. "Then am I right in assuming babies are on the immediate agenda?"

Gabe chuckled as he fondled Izzy's ear. "Let's just say you'll get no argument from me."

Izzy could only sit there, dazed. She already had trouble breathing, and her heart rate was over the moon. Hugo's wild assumption about babies and immediate agendas didn't help matters one bit.

"How exciting!" Hugo clapped his hands. "Perhaps our lovely tropical nights will help matters along?"

"My thinking exactly." She heard the smile in Gabe's voice as he continued to caress her neck, his provoking fingers making her senses reel and leap and spiral. Did he have any idea how unfair, how cruel he was?

Izzy's hand curled around her fork; her brain conjured satisfying images of making mincemeat out of a certain fake husband. *His thinking exactly? Ha!* It was just too bad that doing her boss in with multiple fork wounds would arouse the attention of the others. Initiating Plan B, she kicked him hard with her foot. His grunt let her know he received her message.

"Do let us know when the blessed event occurs." Clara's sweet face beamed with grandmotherly enchantment.

Izzy gulped, too dismayed to form words.

"You're too kind," Gabe said. Izzy heard the slight strain in his voice and knew it was the residue of her kick.

Both Hugo and Clara appeared so delighted about the possibility of a baby, Izzy wanted to run screaming from the whole, awful mess. She hated to lie at all, but compounding the original fabrication with a promise to let them know about a blessed event that was total fabrication, *was unthinkable!*

Gabe stopped stroking her nape to draw near to kiss her temple. Before he withdrew, she heard his barely audible command, *"Smile!"*

Automatically she pasted on a cheerful expression.

Placing an arm around her, he said, "Izzy's shy about discussing such matters in front of other people." He startled her by smoothing back her hair in what appeared to be a loving gesture. "Why don't you pick something else to discuss, darling."

Okay! Let's discuss the pleasure I'll have barbecuing your liver! Though she fumed, Izzy managed to keep her smile pasted on. "Of course, *lambkins,* let me think..." Her cheeks blazed, but she sensed the others would assume she blushed because of embarrassment rather than homicidal urges.

Thankfully the subject moved away from babies. The main dish disappeared. Desserts were served and consumed. And behind a sunny smile, Izzy seethed.

When dinner ended, Hugo and Clara led the party into the drawing room. With a high, decorated ceiling, stately columns and moldings it was a sumptuous and imposing place. As the guests entered, brightly clad servants scurried around rolling up a Persian carpet that dominated the center of the room, leaving the polished hardwood bare.

Gabe tried not to limp as he escorted Izzy inside, but the angry kick she inflicted on his shin throbbed like thunder. He glanced at her, his lips twitching with reluctant mirth. She was mad, the little imp. *She was mad!* He was the casualty, but *she* was mad!

Her expression gave nothing of her anger away, but he could tell. Under his touch her muscles were tight, and her spine had gone ramrod straight. When she suffered a look in his direction, her smile didn't fool him, either. Murder lurked in her eyes.

The band began to tune up.

"We're either going to refinish the floor, or we're in for some dancing," Gabe remarked, trying to draw her into casual conversation.

Izzy nodded at Foxie in greeting, but ignored Gabe.

He took her hand, drawing yet another bloodthirsty glare. "Would you like to sit down?" He indicated a red and gilt sofa, reminiscent of Egypt.

She smiled sweetly. "Why, that's a lovely thought."

He grimaced at her smirk as she seated herself. He joined her on the couch. "My leg is killing me, Peabody."

She smiled, but continued to stare straight ahead. "I'm so pleased, lambkins," she said, loud enough for others to hear.

Hugo turned to grin at them. Izzy smiled and waved, still refusing to face Gabe.

He placed an arm around her so he would be very close when he leaned near her ear. "Why are you so angry?"

She peered at him, but her gaze darted quickly away. After a few heartbeats, she apparently decided to say something, because she shifted to face him. "Why did you have to tell him we were talking about babies?" she demanded between stiffly smiling lips.

"We were."

"And for once you decided to tell the *truth?*"

He had no idea why, but he couldn't suppress a chuckle. "You started it by saying you wanted lots of children."

"I do!"

The band began to play a waltz, and both Gabe and Izzy reflexively glanced up.

Hugo took Clara in his arms and swept her around the floor. Gabe was surprised by how well Hugo waltzed. He seemed more the two-left-feet type. "Now, dear friends," Hugo called out, "I hope a pleasant evening of dancing appeals to you. Clara and I have taken many a ballroom dancing lesson, and we're just vain enough to want to show off."

Izzy cast Gabe a jaundiced look, which he answered with a grin.

"What's so funny," she demanded.

"Peabody, you don't want children. You're much too good at what you do to muddle things up with a husband and babies. Don't be ridiculous."

She stiffened. *"Ridic—"* She must have realized she echoed his word too loudly, for she covered with a coughing fit he knew to be fake. Gabe leaned close and rubbed her back as a doting husband might. She cleared her throat. Though her cheeks glowed with fury, she smiled. *"Ridiculous?* Don't you dare condescend to me, sir! If you have the insane notion—" She cut herself off. For a few seconds her mouth worked as she seemed to try to choose her words. *"Hmmmpt!"* The high-pitched squeak was her only sound as she jerked away to present him with her stiffened profile.

Gabe had a feeling she was so furious she didn't

know how to express what she wanted to say and still hold on to her smile.

He watched her as her gaze followed Hugo and Clara across the dance floor. Foxie and Claudia joined in when the music changed to a current hit song.

Gabe sensed that Peabody agonized to blow their cover, stalk out and let him deal with the aftermath by himself. But as she continued to scan Hugo's animated face, her expression gradually softened. Swallowing hard, she bowed her head. Gabe knew she'd changed her mind.

When she sank back against the cushions, he began to massage her nape. Not so much because he thought he ought to, but because he liked the silky feel of her hair brushing against his hand. When she glanced in his direction, he winked, but her smile remained as false as a politician's promise.

"I've been meaning to tell you something, sir," she said.

He angled his face nearer. Her big eyes glistened and he felt a stab of—of what? Misgiving?

"Yes?"

"Why aren't you two dancing?"

Gabe didn't immediately react. His concentration was centered on Izzy's eyes. Did suffering lurk there, or was it a trick of the mellow light?

Without glancing up, he murmured, "My wife doesn't dance."

"Yes, she does," Izzy corrected, facing Hugo. "I'd love to dance with you."

Gabe was taken off guard by Peabody's abrupt rise from the couch.

Hugo chortled, drawing Gabe's regard. "How is it that your husband doesn't know you dance?"

She tossed Gabe a saucy glance. "Maybe because he never asked." There was no mistaking the glint of defiance in her eyes—mellow lighting or no mellow lighting.

An instant later she sailed off in Hugo's arms, toward the bank of patio doors, thrown wide to welcome the cool night breeze.

Gabe lounged back, watching Peabody skim along the floor with their host. He decided he was wrong about noticing sadness in her eyes a moment ago. There was no trace of it in her demeanor. His prim, no-nonsense *Peabody* swirled and spun in perfect unison with Hugo, as though they were performing on stage. Hugo led her into a dizzying spin, and Gabe hunched forward, staring. At one point, when they swept close by, Izzy eyed Gabe with a contrary smile before she and their host danced away in flawless harmony.

Gabe ran his hand across his jaw, mesmerized. Who was this creature he'd brought here to play his wife, this stranger he thought he knew like a book— from cover to efficient, straitlaced, logical, dull brown cover?

He sank back against the cushion, confused, an emotion he wasn't accustomed to feeling. He clenched his jaws, his glance narrowing as Izzy turned into Hugo's arms for another dramatic spin. Shiny, riotous curls flew around her flushed face and her eyes sparkled with exhilaration. The lighthearted sound of her laughter jolted him, but not unpleasantly. He had no idea Peabody's laughter sounded like that—husky, even seductive.

A curious prickling began at the back of his neck, and he rubbed it.

CHAPTER FIVE

Izzy managed to keep from blowing up at her ever-lastingly amused fake husband until they were safely back in their room. When the door closed, she whirled on him, all primed to tell him she didn't find Hugo's assumption that they were planning to have children—almost any minute—at all funny, and she wanted him to set Hugo straight, immediately. She opened her mouth to speak, but was shocked into silence when he tugged her into his embrace.

"Peabody!" He hugged her against him. "I had no idea you could dance like that! If I'd known you were the Ginger Rogers to Hugo's Fred Astaire, I would never have considered bringing anyone else." His breath was hot against her hair. "The man's so nuts about you, I could insult his baby food, steal his wife and he'd still give me the account."

Pressed against him as she was, Izzy found herself unable to speak or react in any sensible manner—which should have been a punch to his midsection. With her cheek hard against his chest, she couldn't keep from inhaling his scent. His heartbeat was solid and strong in her ear, so unlike hers, *rat-a-tatting* against her rib cage like a jackhammer.

He pressed a kiss on the top of her head, and her legs turned rubbery. "You surprise me." The soft way he made the statement drew her gaze to his.

He searched her face, continuing to hold her. Izzy could feel the sexual magnetism he radiated, and it had its effect. His energy, his potency, thrummed through her, somehow steadying her, giving her an odd kind of strength. But only the strength to look him in the eye and restore her wobbly knees.

A tingling in the pit of her stomach was Izzy's first indication that something had altered in his manner. His smile dimmed. His gaze bore into her in silent appraisal. After a few ticks of the clock, his head canted, as though in preparation for a kiss.

A kiss?

She stared in wonder. She'd often dreamed of feeling those lips fully on hers, possessive, coaxing, driving her wild. Her heart thundered in her ears. Gabriel Parish was so handsome, his appeal so powerful, her good sense was quickly losing ground to her need for him. Wishing she could do anything else—run, scream, kick his shin—she managed only to raise her chin a notch.

Her mind screamed, *Don't, Izzy! The man's a woman magnet! He doesn't know the meaning of the word commitment! You allow this kiss and you won't be able to leave it at that! You'll be lost, but he'll merely roll over in the morning and carve a notch on the bedpost!*

She saw disquiet flash in his eyes, and the sight startled her. His jaw shifted from side to side in what appeared to be unease. Clearing his throat, he slid his hands to her upper arms and moved her away to a safer distance.

"I'd call this a good first day." His grin was again full-blown and sexy. His hands lingered for one more second before he released her. "Good work, Peabody." He patted her shoulder, then headed toward the closet. "I think it's best that we get to sleep. After all that exercise, you must be drained."

She watched him move away with a crazy mixture of relief and sadness. He shrugged his sports coat off broad shoulders and entered the closet to hang it up. With a deep and tremulous inhale, she dragged her gaze from him. She was drained all right, but not from dancing. That had been exhilarating, liberating. No, she was drained emotionally. Drained from the weeks and weeks of vacillation and cowardice. She needed to be away from him, to rid herself of a dream that could never come true. Why couldn't she let herself leave?

With a heavy heart and dragging steps she turned away. "Isabel Peabody," she muttered. "You're a lily-livered chicken. When are you going to face up to what you have to do?"

Grabbing some night things from a drawer, she escaped to the bath. This couldn't go on. He had actually taken her into his arms, and he'd even thought of kissing her. She'd seen it in his eyes, though the urge passed before he'd followed through. But what if he *had?* What if, for some unknown reason, he *did* kiss her. Maybe when Hugo gave him the account? Her boss was a demonstrative man. He might unthinkingly grab her and plant a hot one right on her lips. What would she do then—follow him around like an adoring puppy for the rest of her life?

When she was safely behind the bathroom door, she sagged against it. "You will *not,* Izzy," she grumbled. "You will *not* let that happen, even if you have to run shrieking into the sea!"

Gabe shed his clothes and donned a green pair of boxer-style shorts. Accustomed to sleeping in the raw, he didn't have many choices. Surely Peabody had seen men in swimsuits, and wouldn't be immoderately outraged.

Strolling onto the balcony, he inhaled the sea breeze, chuckling at his mistaken impression of his little assistant. He'd thought he knew her so completely, yet he hadn't had a clue that she could dance. Hadn't even considered that she had a ripe figure under those boxy suits she'd always worn. Hadn't realized her hair was quite so—so velvety, or imagined how it flashed with fire when bouncing around her face.

Neither had he guessed her laughter was so husky and stimulating, or that her animated expression and smile could do things to...

A tightening in his gut caused his grin to fade. He also had never considered the notion that he would feel any desire to—

Biting back a curse, he gripped the metal rail. Peabody was *not* a woman to him. She was more than that. Women were interchangeable, replaceable. Peabody was essential. She had a good, sharp mind and ran his office like a top sergeant, anticipating his orders before he even knew what he wanted.

He clenched his fists around the cool metal. "I will not screw up a perfect working relationship simply because her laugh..."

He winced and reached up to rub that annoying prickle at the back of his neck. What it was and why it had come on tonight, he didn't know. Probably a reaction to a tropical pollen or mold spore. He worked his shoulders and arched his back. He was tight. Most likely tension from the trip and the tough competition.

As he turned around and propped a hip against the railing, the bed snagged his gaze. He eyed the thing, concerned. He'd had every intention of platonically sharing that puny mattress with Peabody. The idea of anything physical going on between them had no more entered his head than if he'd planned to sleep beside his briefcase.

Until now.

He dipped his head, feeling like an awkward schoolboy. A cool breeze informed him that his brow had broken out in a sweat. He supposed his unprofessional turn of mind was natural, under the circumstances. He'd been busy lately, preoccupied with the Yum-Yum campaign, among others. He'd gone without female companionship way too long. That was his problem. Peabody was his right arm, his hardworking, loyal associate, not a good-for-now girl, worthy of only a night or two of lust.

A door creaked open and his glance shot to the bath entrance. She came out wearing a flowing black negligee and matching peignoir. The creation covered her from her throat to her toes, and was made of a fairly opaque fabric. Unfortunately for his state of mind, the instant she stepped before the bedside lamp, a shadowy impression of feminine curves became all too evident.

Gabe closed his eyes and issued up a prayer for strength. His high-minded, faithful Peabody didn't deserve what he was thinking.

At first Izzy didn't see him, then stumbled to a halt when she did. He was on the balcony. Golden light filtering out from the bedside lamp illuminated his torso, muscular and tempting. Her scrutiny moved helplessly down over slim male hips and long, athletic legs. With a mighty force of will, she cut short her unruly inspection and dragged her attention to his face. His eyes were closed and he looked as if he might have a headache. Well, that was too bad, because she was going to make it worse. She could no longer abide the situation as it stood.

"Mr. Parish?"

He opened his eyes and seemed to wince. Yes, he definitely had a headache. She marched to her purse and yanked out her resignation letter. Stalking with it to the balcony, she held out a stiff arm. "I quit."

He frowned, as though he didn't think he'd heard right. His glance shifted from the paper to her face, but otherwise he didn't speak or move.

Unable to go on standing there being glowered at, she let the letter slip to the balcony floor and pivoted around so she wouldn't have to bear the torment of looking at him. "I can't stand this trickery." She struggled to keep her voice even. The part about the trickery was true, but the heart of the matter—the main reason she had to leave him—wasn't something she would ever admit out loud. She would suffer the tortures of the damned first. "I need to make some changes in my life, sir, and this—this *fiction* to get Hugo Rufus's account is the last straw."

A moment passed when Izzy could hear nothing but the rush of the surf and the rustle of palmetto leaves in the breeze. The sounds, usually considered calming, did nothing to ease the knot that had formed in her stomach. She swallowed several times, wishing he would say something. Anything. Even anger would be better than this suffocating silence.

"You're kidding," he finally whispered, not sounding particularly amused.

She shook her head. *Coward!* she chided inwardly. *Look the man in the eye. Show him you mean business!*

She heard his approach across the wooden floor. When he took hold of her upper arms, she tensed. *No! No fair touching!*

He turned her to face him. He wasn't smiling; his eyes weren't twinkling. "Peabody, this ruse isn't doing Hugo any harm. Only good. Don't you understand that? He needs what I can offer him." His lips lifted in a reassuring smile as he slid an arm around her. "You like the man and so do I. If he gives us the account, there's no way either he or Yum-Yum could lose." He squeezed her, she feared, more for emphasis than affection. "You want him to be happy, don't you?" Izzy cast him a mistrustful look, aware that he was working her. "You've seen some of what I want to do for him, haven't you?" She frowned, trying not to be drawn in, yet her glance doggedly roamed his face.

He smiled, recounting the ideas he'd formulated for Hugo, ideas that would make Yum-Yum the bestselling baby food in the country. Izzy knew she was a fool to let him spin his web, but she couldn't help being affected. Witnessing his passion sparkling in his eyes, put fractures in her brick-wall stance to quit. As she watched and listened, she was reminded again that he didn't do this for money or prestige, but for the excitement of conceiving an idea and seeing it through.

Ironically, the way he felt about his work was exactly like her desire to give birth. That reminder bolstered her determination, and she fought against falling under his spell. She could understand his excitement about his profession, but she could no longer share it—didn't dare.

If she let him talk her into staying, one day she would wake up and discover twenty-five years had sailed by. Izzy Peabody would still be Gabriel Parish's assistant, with nothing in her life but a full schedule and an empty heart.

Breaking out of his hold, she hurried onto the balcony and scooped up the letter. Stony-faced, she thrust it into his hand. "This is no joke, sir."

Gabe's features darkened. She spun to go, but he grasped her wrist. "Your stubbornness is beginning to annoy me, Peabody." Crumpling the letter, he tossed it to the floor. "Go ahead and let off a little steam, if you have to. When you calm down, you'll regain your senses."

She yanked from his grasp. "I'm *perfectly* calm!" That wasn't true. However, at the moment, being calm had nothing to do with her ability to make rational decisions about what was good for her mental health and what wasn't. Being close to Gabe every day was definitely not! Rubbing away the tingling remnants of his touch, she stomped to the bed and threw back the covers. "There's nothing more to say."

She made the mistake of shifting to scowl at him. Her heart leapt absurdly. He stood in the mellow lamplight scowling back, fists on hips, legs braced wide—the image of an Indian warrior out of America's past.

The night breeze nudged a dark lock of hair across his furrowed brow as though blatantly provoking her, making her crave the chance to finger-stroke it back, to know the reckless joy of being held in Gabriel Parish's arms, of seeing passion *for her* in his eyes.

With effort she looked away and crawled under the light covers. She lay stiffly, on the edge of the mattress, in order to put as much distance between them as possible. His taunting threat to share the bed echoed in her brain, and she squeezed her eyes shut, trying to block out the memory of his voice, erase from her mind the teasing glint in his eyes.

"Peabody."

Her name had been spoken softly and from no farther away than a few inches. Izzy jumped, nearly tumbling out of bed. Gabe caught her by the shoulders and settled her back. He knelt beside her. She had no idea how he'd approached so soundlessly. Perhaps there was a touch of Indian warrior in him, after all.

His expression was one of aggravated tolerance. "What things need changing so badly in your life?" He surprised her and took her hand. "Maybe I can help change them so you won't leave me."

She pulled from his grasp and buried her hand beneath the covers. "There's nothing you can do." She found it hard to speak. His lips were too close, his breath warm and delicious against her face.

She was sure if he knew the truth, he would burst out laughing, then insist, under *those* circumstances, leaving would be for the best. She couldn't endure such humiliation and heartbreak. "Would you give me children?" Dismayed, she bit her lip. That slipped out without her consent! She watched his face, hoping he wouldn't take it the way she meant it.

His eyes widened a fraction. "What?"

The hushed, incredulous tone sent a cold wave of

depression washing over her. It was painfully clear the idea had never crossed his mind. "I mean—I want a husband and children. *A family.* Working for you, I have no social life. I don't blame you. You are the way you are." She hated the wistfulness in her voice. "You work eighty hours a week and you love every minute of it. But being your assistant is not fulfilling enough for me."

After a moment, one corner of his mouth twisted upward. "Don't talk foolishness. Advertising is in your blood. You couldn't be as good as you are if you weren't meant to—"

"You're wrong," she cut in. "Don't try to talk me into staying. I have to go."

A thoughtful frown flitted across his features. For the first time he seemed to sense that he might not be able to cajole her into thinking his way. "Don't do this, Peabody. What would I do without you?"

Izzy was struck by the irony of his question. There he was, kneeling by her bedside, sounding like a husband devastated that his beloved wife has decided to leave him. The only difference was, he called her Peabody, not darling or even Izzy! Grief overwhelmed her and she had to turn away. "I'll stay out the week, Mr. Parish," she said, her wretchedness hard to hide. "But when we get back to New York, I'm gone."

For the next two days, numerous activities threw Izzy and Gabe together in the guise of a loving man and wife. Both of them were angry, now, making the intimacies of tender looks and fond touches difficult to carry out.

Izzy's emotions were in tatters. She cringed at their

empty familiarities—of Gabe's warm hand continually at her waist or his fingers entwined with hers. She hated her heart-pounding reaction to sharing close quarters, with his scent lingering in the air, mocking her, filling her head and her fitful dreams.

Though Gabe laughed and smiled and appeared the carefree guest, deep in his eyes she saw his frustration. She was positive that nobody in his past, either personally or professionally, had ever voluntarily left him. He was infuriated at the very notion that she, of all his dependable office accoutrements, would dare such insubordination.

Izzy hardly slept, though miraculously Gabe didn't join her in bed as he'd threatened. He had taken to sitting across the room, working on his presentation until the wee hours. Izzy knew he eventually fell asleep there, for she woke often from disturbing dreams to see him lounging in the chair—sleeping—his legs stretched out, ankles crossed, his head supported by the wall.

She tried not to watch him. Not to dwell on his firm lips or the way his tanned skin stretched appealingly over high cheekbones. She avoided examining his lean, athletic body, powerful chest and long, long legs. Thinking back on it now, she had a sinking feeling she had failed badly in her vow to ignore him.

Izzy marveled at how he could cope with sitting up all night in a Sheraton chair, too stiff and skimpy to be comfortable, especially for a man his size. She was amazed that he looked alert and rested each day. Of course, he was the type who thrived on four hours of sleep. It astounded her that he appeared to be the epitome of a contented husband—except when she looked deep in his eyes and witnessed the inferno raging there.

On Wednesday, the group went picnicking in a secluded cove. Tranquillity Island was a place of endless sun and boundless reserves of white sand beaches. Turquoise water glistened offshore as the ocean's fingertips trailed lazily along the beach in whispery caresses. As a backdrop for their outing, the pristine woodland stood, a silent, green sentry. Foothills led to the craggy volcanic peak, where odd granite formations created a magical play of light and dark before probing upward into the clouds.

Hugo was his usual bubbly self, dashing around to pour iced tea while personally barbecuing the steaks. Now he sat cross-legged in the shade, weaving a straw hat out of grasses. This one he'd promised to Izzy. He'd pledged that before the week was through, he would have one for every guest. So far Hedda and Roger Miles had been presented with theirs. No doubt Hugo decided with their pale skin, they needed protection immediately. The Chicago couple peered out from behind a salt grass fringe, looking as awkward as ever, and totally out of place.

Watching Hugo roost there, humming to himself and weaving, occasionally hopping up to make sure no glass was empty on his watch, Izzy could only smile. Though the Wirts made derogatory comments behind his back, and the Mileses were clearly less than delighted by their surroundings, every sweet, oddball thing Hugo did lifted Izzy's mood a notch—except when she chanced to look at Gabe.

He had his ever-present notebook out, sporadically recording thoughts and ideas. His Yum-Yum presentation was scheduled for tomorrow morning, and Izzy knew he was still tweaking and adjusting his concept.

Seated in comfortable wicker that had been set out for the party, Izzy was startled from her musings when Clara took the chair beside her and held out a plate of coconut crisps. "Have you tried these?"

Izzy nodded and took one of the long thin pieces of baked coconut. "I'd love another, thank you." She felt a pang of guilt. The quiet woman was so gentle and sweet-natured, Izzy hated that she wasn't who Clara thought she was.

Her hostess smiled. "You look wonderful. Your cheeks are so flushed with health."

Izzy knew her cheeks were flushed, but with crushing guilt. She took a bite of the crisp and chanced a peek at Gabe. He stared toward the ocean, but she knew he wasn't seeing it. All his energy, his whole being, was centered on work.

Clara leaned close. "I can tell you like my Hugo."

Izzy glanced at him, weaving and humming, and she grinned. Genuinely grinned. Hugo wore baggy mattress-ticking shorts and a yellow T-shirt with a huge smiley face on the front. His own handmade straw hat was tipped back so far on his head it looked as if he sported a shaggy halo. "He's wonderful." She faced Clara. "A truly special human being. So openhearted and loving."

It was Clara's turn to blush. "There was a time when he was nothing like the man you see now."

"Really?" Izzy was thunderstruck. "How can that be?"

Clara's smile faded. "I went to work for Hugo after my husband died. I'd been a secretary until my boys were born. When Raymond passed away, both our sons were in college. I needed a job, and Hugo needed a secretary. He paid extremely well, but he was a driven man. A tyrant to work for.''

"No." Izzy stared at Hugo. "Not him."

"Oh, yes. He worked a twenty-hour day and expected his employees to do so, too."

"But—but he's not that way, now." Izzy frowned in confusion. "What changed him?"

"The heart attack." Clara cast her husband a loving glance. "It almost killed him. I was the only person to visit him in the hospital. You see, I'd found out much to my surprise that I'd grown to care deeply for the man, though I knew getting involved with him on a personal level would be virtual suicide. He had no room in his life for family—or even friends."

Izzy felt a stab of identification.

"One day while visiting him, I was reading some of my favorite poetry aloud. He touched my face." Clara's blush returned. "He smiled and thanked me for being kind to a brute like him. When I tried to object, he went on to tell me that he'd had to work since he was seven years old. He'd never had a childhood, and he hadn't made time for a family. I'll never forget that moment," she said. "He was crying and he said, 'Clara, I don't want to die without ever having lived. Will you marry me?'"

Tears shimmered in Clara's eyes, and Izzy felt a tickle in her nose. She knew her own eyes would soon fill up. "How—how sweet." Izzy could see painful parallels between Hugo's earlier existence and her present one.

Clara blinked back the moisture. "Hugo was a changed man from that day on. He turned a good portion of Yum-Yum's administrative duties over to subordinates. We took a year-long honeymoon, traveling around the world. That's how we found this island.'' She touched Izzy's hand. ''When I was cleaning out some old file cabinets in the office, I found one filled with all the baby pictures that had been sent over the years. Hugo had never seen them, and was so touched, he insisted on displaying them in our home.'' She sniffed and shook her head. ''He would have loved to have had children of his own, poor dear.''

Izzy turned toward Hugo, experiencing a tug of pity. So that's why the photographs meant so much. She hadn't been wrong when she'd thought she'd seen a glimmer of vulnerability in his eyes that day he'd told them about ''his family.'' ''What about his heart?'' She looked at Clara, new anxiety billowing. ''He seems so healthy.''

''Oh, yes. He's a happy man, now. Without all that stress, he's as healthy as a horse. And he's taken on my sons and their children as though they were his own. Every summer, all four grandchildren spend the month of July here.''

Clara squeezed Izzy's wrist, her attention moving to Gabe, writing in his notebook. ''Your husband is brilliant and charming.'' Her expression changed slightly and Izzy sensed concern. ''I hope he knows how important family is. He seems somewhat preoccupied with work.''

Clara was perceptive. She knew Gabe was like the old Hugo, driven, oblivious to the fact that life was passing him by. It had taken Izzy three years in his employ to realize the same thing was happening to her. Ironically, before she'd joined his fast-paced world, she'd disdained her mother's choice to be a housewife, thinking being stuck at home a horrible, boring fate.

She now understood the fast lane could be an empty, arid existence, rushing you along, not allowing for meaningful relationships or loving bonds. She'd learned her mother was right, all along. Izzy realized Granny Dorie had passed on that wisdom to Izzy's mother, years ago. What a shame that when her own mother tried to teach her that truth, Izzy had been too headstrong to listen.

Izzy's throat closed and she faced Clara. She didn't know what to say. After all, she had no real influence over Gabe.

The older woman patted Izzy's hand, her smile kind. "Don't let him work for the next three decades only to wake up to the fact that his family doesn't know him and he has no friends."

Izzy visualized Gabriel Parish having a heart attack in thirty years—alone. The vision stabbed deep, puncturing her heart. Gabe was so much more like the old Hugo than she. He lived a hell-bent-for-leather existence—blindly rushing onward, onward, allowing worthwhile human attachments to slip through his fingers. Though he didn't see Izzy as a woman—let alone a potential mate—her heart turned over with a desire to help the man she loved avoid the same barren fate Hugo almost succumbed to.

She cast another glance toward Gabe. His fixed expression told her he witnessed nothing of the sparkling sea or the warm, white beach. His mind was wholly fixed on the meeting he was to have with Hugo. Business—always business. Every few minutes he would seem to come awake, only to scribble something in his spiral, unaware of the paradise surrounding him.

Izzy had a sudden brainstorm and turned to Clara. "Will you excuse me? I think my husband could use a little diversion."

Clara smiled and nodded. "You'll be a good influence on him, dear. I can tell."

As Izzy pushed up from her chair she knew Clara was right. She definitely would. In the time she had left to influence her workaholic boss, she would do her best to free him, make him learn that "fun" was *not* a four-letter word.

Sauntering over to his chair, she smiled impishly. "Hello—*honey.*" He blinked and glanced up. His expression held just enough blankness to show her that he wasn't quite out of his imagination yet. She took the opportunity to pluck his notebook from his fingers and dash toward the surf. "Catch me, *sugar pie!*" With a mischievous laugh, she wagged the notebook high in the air. "We're going to get all wet, unless you can catch us first!"

Gabe's startled expression narrowed as he focused on his waylaid notebook, heading toward a watery demise.

She could almost hear him thinking, *What are you doing, Peabody? Have you lost your senses?*

No, my oblivious love, she threw back telepathically, *I'm trying to help you come to yours!*

When he vaulted from his chair, his long strides ate up the distance. Experiencing a mixture of anticipation and panic, Izzy's heart tripped over itself. She bolted into the surf. When water swirled around her thighs, her lead diminished alarmingly.

Since her plan had been to taunt him into having a

PLAY...

"ROLL A DOUBLE!"

PEEL OFF LABEL AND PLACE INSIDE

GET 2 BOOKS

AND A

FABULOUS MYSTERY BONUS GIFT

ABSOLUTELY FREE!

SEE INSIDE...

(H-R-07/00)

NO RISK, NO OBLIGATION TO BUY...NOW OR EVER!

GUARANTEED

PLAY "ROLL A DOUBLE" AND YOU GET FREE GIFTS! HERE'S HOW TO PLAY:

1. Peel off label from front cover. Place it in space provided at right. With a coin, carefully scratch off the silver dice. Then check the claim chart to see what we have for you – TWO FREE BOOKS and a mystery gift – ALL YOURS! ALL FREE!

2. Send back this card and you'll receive brand-new Harlequin Romance® novels. These books have a cover price of $3.50 each in the U.S. and $3.99 each in Canada, but they are yours to keep absolutely free.

3. There's no catch. You're under no obligation to buy anything. We charge nothing – ZERO – for your first shipment. And you don't have to make any minimum number of purchases – not even one!

4. The fact is, thousands of readers enjoy receiving books by mail from the Harlequin Reader Service®. They like the convenience of home delivery...they like getting the best new novels BEFORE they're available in stores...and they love our discount prices!

5. We hope that after receiving your free books you'll want to remain a subscriber. But the choice is yours – to continue or cancel any time at all! So why not take us up on our invitation, with no risk of any kind. You'll be glad you did!

THIS MYSTERY BONUS GIFT
WILL BE YOURS __FREE__ WHEN
YOU PLAY "ROLL A DOUBLE"

"ROLL A DOUBLE!"

Place label here

SCRATCH HERE

SEE CLAIM CHART BELOW

316 HDL CQVU

116 HDL CQVE
(H-R-07/99)

YES! I have placed my label from the front cover into the space provided above and scratched off the silver dice to reveal a double. Please send me all the gifts for which I qualify. I understand that I am under no obligation to purchase any books, as explained on the back and on the opposite page.

Name:
                     (PLEASE PRINT)

Address: Apt.#:

City: State/Prov.:   Zip/ Postal Code:

CLAIM CHART

🎲🎲	**2 FREE BOOKS PLUS MYSTERY BONUS GIFT**
🎲🎲	**2 FREE BOOKS**
🎲🎲	**1 FREE BOOK**

CLAIM NO.37-829

PRINTED IN U.S.A.

The Harlequin Reader Service® — Here's how it works:

Accepting your 2 free books and mystery gift places you under no obligation to buy anything. You may keep the books and gift and return the shipping statement marked "cancel." If you do not cancel, about a month later we'll send you 6 additional novels and bill you just $2.90 each in the U.S., or $3.34 each in Canada, plus 25¢ delivery per book and applicable taxes if any.* That's the complete price and — compared to the cover price of $3.50 in the U.S. and $3.99 in Canada — it's quite a bargain! You may cancel at any time, but if you choose to continue, every month we'll send you 6 more books, which you may either purchase at the discount price or return to us and cancel your subscription.

*Terms and prices subject to change without notice. Sales tax applicable in N.Y. Canadian residents will be charged applicable provincial taxes and GST.

If offer card is missing write to: Harlequin Reader Service, 3010 Walden Ave., P.O. Box 1867, Buffalo NY 14240-1867

BUSINESS REPLY MAIL
FIRST-CLASS MAIL   PERMIT NO. 717   BUFFALO, NY

POSTAGE WILL BE PAID BY ADDRESSEE

HARLEQUIN READER SERVICE
3010 WALDEN AVE
PO BOX 1867
BUFFALO NY 14240-9952

NO POSTAGE
NECESSARY
IF MAILED
IN THE
UNITED STATES

little fun, she held the notebook high. She had no intention of destroying his dratted ''mind tablet'' as he called it. However, now that she was far out in the water, wearing only a bathing suit, what did she think she was going to do with it? As soon as he was upon her, he needed only to snatch it and the game would be over.

''Give me that—*darling*,'' Gabe said, his guise of ''affectionate husband'' slipping a little. She couldn't miss the flash of annoyance in his eyes.

''No!'' In a fit of insanity, she stuffed it down the back of her suit. ''I want to play.''

''You want to play, do you?'' His lips twisted in a cynical smile. ''What's with you, Peabody?''

''I'm going to dive!''

He grabbed her waist. ''Not likely.''

''I'll dunk myself! You can't stop me!''

''You're not going anyplace.'' He cupped her hips in his hands and lifted her so she had to clench his waist with her thighs or fall backward. As soon as her legs were fastened around him she realized it was a bad mistake. She gulped, flustered.

His grin gave him the look of a cunning wolf, and his eyes sparked with triumph. ''Don't make me dig for it, Peabody.''

Irritated that he assumed victory so easily, she balked. ''If I don't give it back, what are you going to do, fire me?''

''What I'd do might shock you.'' A brow rose, the small act strangely threatening. ''Give me the book.''

She grinned, not sure what there was to be smug about. Maybe it was because she knew her boss was a gentleman, and he wouldn't do her harm. In a lightning-strike move, motivated by some demented feminine impulse, she retrieved the notebook and shoved it down the front of her suit. With a mischievous giggle, she slid her arms around his neck. "I dare you—*darling.*"

Plainly startled, Gabe's gaze raked over her bodice then lifted to her face. Droplets of spray twinkled in his hair and on his lashes. She grew transfixed by the masculine beauty of his features and the hard texture of his body, sturdy beneath her touch.

He was riveting, tempting, but she fiercely resisted her need to lift her mouth to his, touch those full, male lips and die of happiness. Facing the fact that she was getting a little crazy, she decided she'd better separate herself from him. She loosened her grip with her legs.

"*No!*" His hands cupping her hips, tightened possessively.

"No?" She was confused and suddenly breathless. Her mind sputtered and misfired. What could he possibly mean by *no?*

His eyes were hooded, his features unreadable. Yet, there was something in his manner that made her skin tingle pleasantly.

"Peabody..." Her name was a husky murmur. "I think it's time we kiss."

CHAPTER SIX

KISS?

Izzy had a quick vision of her dismal, haunted future if she let *that* happen. She flew into a panic, pushed at his chest and sprang from his hold, hoping the act looked playful.

Staggering to get a foothold on loose sand, she whipped his notepad from her bodice and gave it a hearty toss toward shore. When she could tell it would make dry sand, she flung herself away from Gabe in a shallow dive. The water felt like ice against her flaming skin. She swam as though a demon snapped at her heels, knowing only that she had to get away from Gabe and his wicked deceptions. A public kiss was going too far. *She'd already told him that!*

A sudden restraint at her ankle made her cry out; but to her ears all she heard was a gurgley grunt.

Her hair swirled forward around her face, and she could tell she was being pulled backward. Since she didn't like opening her eyes in saltwater, she couldn't see what held her, but it didn't take much imagination to figure it out. Since she hadn't seen signs of marauding sharks, she had a feeling it was less likely to be a Great White than another kind of shark. The business kind.

She kicked and struggled to break the grip, but he was having none of it. Sputtering she broke the surface and twisted around, wiping her eyes. Sure enough, Gabe clutched her leg with one hand. He wasn't quite grinning, but mischief twinkled in his eyes.

She kicked her captured leg, trying vainly to break his hold. "What are you doing!"

"I'm playing with my wife. I thought that's what you wanted?"

He hauled her toward him. Caught by surprise, she went under. With her free foot, she felt around desperately for solid purchase on the bottom. She failed. Resurfacing, she coughed and gasped. Peering at him through one stinging eye, she choked out, "I thought—you wanted—your notebook."

"It's fine for now."

"I'm happy for *it!*" Since she couldn't find the bottom or get away, she kicked water at him. "Let go of my leg!"

He took most of the liquid in the face. Spitting seawater, he wiped his eyes. "Oh, no you don't." His roguish grin returned. "It's playtime—*darling.*"

He grabbed her free leg and she fought like a marlin on a fisherman's line. To her dismay, his grasp held. He dragged her legs around him, so she straddled his middle, again.

"I liked you where you were." His eyes glinted with meaning.

Alarmed, she twisted her upper body facedown in the water. She wasn't sure how this would help, except that she couldn't clamp her legs around his waist from this position. Not unless she planned to break a few important bones. In the space of a heartbeat, Gabe released her ankles and curled strong arms around her middle, hauling her to him, her back crushed against his chest. She squealed, and suspected those on shore assumed they were having fun.

If the truth were told, she came out of the water smiling. What was that all about? Her traitorous lips had no business curving *up!* She redoubled her efforts to get away, struggling and kicking, squealing and giggling! *Giggling?* Heaven only knew where that reprehensible sound came from!

Gabe's lips grazed her ear. "This playing idea was great, Peabody. I'm glad to see you're getting into the spirit."

His breath warmed her wet flesh. An insubordinate quiver rushed through her, cutting off her ability to deny that this "play" had anything to do with getting into the spirit of their sham!

"Why didn't you let me kiss you?" He nipped her earlobe, and shivers of delight cavorted along her spine.

"I told you I don't like the idea," she said raggedly as his arms locked more securely beneath her breasts. While she thrashed, her foolish body recorded every detail of where his warm, hard flesh touched hers, of his coiled strength and the silky feel of hair on his forearms and chest. He was all man. And too powerful to escape from. She knew that, and so did he.

"You should learn to like the idea of kissing me, *darling.*" His dastardly lips tickled her ear as he spoke. "It's going to happen."

"Don't you *dare!*" A preposterous giggle escaped her throat, undermining her warning.

"It's for show, Peabody. I think it's necessary."

"It's *not* necessary." This time she managed to keep her tone stern. "Put me down!"

"What'll you give me if I do?"

"I'll give you something if you *don't.*"

His chuckle rumbled through her, way too pleasantly. The rat!

"Threats, Peabody?"

She wrestled without success, kicking up a froth. "Don't make me have to get *physical*." She was laughing outright now. How stupid could she be, luxuriating in her imprisonment? The man's life was his career. This marriage conspiracy only proved how one-tracked he was.

"You? Get physical?" Amusement was ripe in his voice. "Wouldn't that put us on the same side of this argument?"

His arms tightened possessively, his lips moving lower to feast on her throat. As though he'd flipped an On/Off switch, her legs went slack. *"Oh…"*

He chuckled, his tongue and teeth making her body react in unruly ways.

"Don't…" she breathed, twisting to make pleading eye contact. "Please!" The word came out in a fragile whisper.

He lifted his head; his grin faded. He grew blurry, and she had to blink to clear her vision.

Gritting a curse, he let her go. When Izzy's feet touched sand, she was so unsteady she sank to her knees. Only her head and shoulders were visible.

With a wry grin and a slight frown between his brows, Gabe dropped to his knees, too. "Mind if I slide between your legs?"

"What?" It came out in an incredulous squeak.

He laughed, but without much humor. "I mean, let me set you on my shoulders. At least we can come out of the water looking like we're having fun."

Though numb with the trouncing her emotions had

taken from contact with his body, she understood and nodded.

"Remember, Peabody, this was your idea." His eyes took on the same frustrated heat she was becoming accustomed to seeing. Before she could respond, he slipped beneath the surface. After a few seconds she gasped as he came up between her legs, hoisting her on his shoulders.

Once he'd risen to his feet, he began to stride toward shore. *"Giggle!"* he whispered. "We're supposed to be having a good time."

He burst out in a booming laugh that sounded real, but Izzy knew it was as artificial as the display they'd just put on.

Gabe could now *absolutely* put his finger on the reason he'd pressed the kiss issue with Peabody, yesterday. He'd given it a lot of thought and he concluded that, at the time, he'd believed they needed to show their affections more strongly. That was the reason.

The only reason.

Furthermore, he was *not* bothered in the least that she resisted so completely. Good Lord, you would have thought he was trying to kidnap her and sell her into a harem.

"What did you say, Gabe, boy?"

Gabe looked up from the advertising storyboard he'd been explaining to Hugo. "What?"

"You said, kiss me." Hugo wagged his white eyebrows puckishly. "I like you, son, but there's a limit."

Gabe clenched his teeth. *Where the hell was his mind?* Here he was, in the middle of his Yum-Yum pitch, overrun with thoughts of Peabody—unable to yank from his mind the warmth and smoothness of her skin, the feminine curve of her bottom. His hands still tingled with the memory of—

He cleared his throat, shifting in his chair. "Sorry, Hugo." With an effort, he grinned. "I'm afraid my thoughts drifted to my little—Izzy…" That outrageous truth was the only thing he could come up with. Apparently his explanation was satisfactory, because Hugo beamed.

"She's a remarkable, remarkable woman." The older man nodded emphatically, his white hair a wispy platinum radiance around his pate. "I don't blame you for being preoccupied with her, my boy." He pointed to the storyboard. "So after that rock band plays that new Yum-Yum theme, then what?"

Gabe went on with his presentation, forcing himself to pay attention to his job. Blast it, he was going to win this account! Not to mention, the millions in revenue would be a nice bonus. He had to get his priorities straight. To Hades with his silly, soft thinking about Peabody, no matter how sensual she was gradually showing herself to be, day by surprising day.

He squelched another urge to mentally wander away from the task at hand. There was absolutely *no* need for him to kiss her. He must have gotten too much sun, or he was under more stress about this account than he realized, or he was balmy from trying to sleep in that damnable chair. It was one or more of those three things.

And that was all it was.

That evening as Izzy walked into dinner beside Gabe, she noticed Hugo wasn't his usual animated self. He sat stiffly, his eyes downcast, at the head of the big table. Izzy experienced a flutter of trepidation. Though she and Gabe were hardly close confidants, she touched his elbow. "Something's wrong."

Gabe nodded imperceptibly, but made no comment. A servant met them inside the door and showed them to their places. Tonight they were seated across from each other, rather than side by side. The Mileses sat on Izzy's side of the table while Foxie and Claudia Wirt had been seated on the side with Gabe.

After taking her place, Izzy smiled at the Mileses and then the Wirts. Both couples acknowledged her with forced expressions of pleasure. Izzy tensed, clasping her fists together in her lap.

She looked at Gabe, stared into his eyes. For some reason, watching him watch her gave her strength, which was idiotic. Still, no matter how absurd their relationship had become, he was the only person in the room she could look to for emotional support. That thought, too, was idiotic. Emotional support? Mr. Don't-Talk-Foolishness Parish?

She shifted toward Hugo. He sat without moving, so unlike him. His eyes looked closed from her vantage point. Izzy experienced a wave of foreboding. What was the matter? Had this advertising campaign idea come too late? Was his empire crumbling around him? He seemed so despondent. Izzy looked at Clara. She, too, seemed uncomfortable, unable to make eye contact.

Izzy swallowed. Her throat was dry. Their water goblets were full and inviting, but Izzy didn't dare reach for hers. She was so overwrought with worry she feared the crystal would slip from her fingers, shattering all over the damask cloth.

Izzy sucked in a long breath, praying it wasn't too

late for Hugo and the Yum-Yum company, with its thousands upon thousands of employees. Her eyes filled with empathetic tears and she blinked hard to stem the rising tide of emotion.

A ringing sound lifted her glance toward Hugo. He tapped his water goblet with a silver spoon. "Excuse me, everybody." He rapped again. The ringing of silver against crystal filled the air, sounding excessively loud in the stillness.

Hugo took his time to lower the spoon to the table. When he finally did, he cleared his throat. He lifted his gaze to face his guests with what looked like monumental effort. Izzy chewed her lip, racked with dread. *Please don't let him tell us he's bankrupt! Please don't let this wonderful man be destitute.*

"Ladies and gentlemen..." Hugo's voice was tremulous. "I have unhappy news." He scanned the diners slowly, face by face, before returning his anguished gaze to his plate. "Today some information came to me which was painful to hear—or accept."

Izzy watched Hugo with a mixture of fear and compassion. She would give anything to keep him from having to make his admission of failure.

"It seems," Hugo went on, "we have a charlatan in our midst."

Izzy's breath froze in her lungs. *A charlatan in our midst!* She grew light-headed with shame as waves of gray passed before her eyes. At the terrifying prospect of being unmasked *and despised* by this kind, generous man, she shot Gabe a tormented look.

His expression betrayed no emotion. With the slight lift of his chin, he seemed to counsel—*take what comes with dignity and grace.*

Yes. He was right. Her apology would be heartfelt,

then she and Gabe would quietly leave. It was bad enough to be discovered as frauds, but to be ejected whining and whimpering would only add to their dishonor.

Izzy forced herself to face Hugo squarely as he scanned his guests. "An hour ago, I received a call from a person calling herself Mrs. Wirt, tracking down her estranged husband about a delinquent child support payment." Hugo's glance shifted to Foxie, now beet red and squirming. "I was told in no uncertain terms that you are *not* married to Claudia." His solemn gaze shifted briefly to the blonde. "That you have dishonored the sanctity of your marriage, abandoned monetary support of your legal wife and children, and are my guest under false colors—with your mistress."

Izzy couldn't believe what she was hearing. It took all her fortitude not to slide to the floor in a relieved heap. She and Gabe were not the frauds being unmasked, after all! Though their reprieve was nothing less than miraculous, she couldn't banish the stone of guilt lodged in her chest.

Izzy was only minimally aware when Claudia bolted from the table and ran sobbing from the room. She heard Foxie do some mewling and blathering, but in the end, he, too, left. However, not before being given instructions from Hugo that the couple be prepared to depart the island at first light via the mail boat.

After Foxie and Claudia were gone, Hugo, bless his heart, tried to regain his breezy mood, but she could tell he was badly wounded by the deception. Izzy couldn't taste the spicy roast pork, couldn't track the dinner conversation for more than a few seconds at a time. Her heart ached with culpability. She and Gabe were every bit as guilty as the Wirts, er, Foxie and Claudia. She and her boss had simply been luckier, with no estranged spouses hunting them down.

Once, when Gabe caught her eye, he lifted his brows and grinned, reminding her to smile, to join in, but her heart was too heavy. This horrible revelation brought home full force just how dastardly she and Gabe were behaving.

"Are you feeling ill?" Hugo touched Izzy's hand, startling her from her troubled thoughts.

She smiled weakly, wishing she deserved his solicitude. Mindful that she couldn't sustain her composure much longer, she nodded. "I—I'm afraid I have a headache." It was no lie. Her head was pounding.

"Darling?" Gabe pushed up from the table, glancing apologetically at their host. "Please excuse us. I must see to my wife."

Hugo and Roger stood as Gabe played the devoted husband, assisting Izzy from her chair.

"I hope you feel better, dear," Clara said. "If you'd like something to eat later, don't hesitate to ring."

"I—I will."

Gabe encircled Izzy's waist with a supportive arm as Izzy made reluctant eye contact with Clara and managed the barest of smiles. She felt hot and cold and shaky and contemptible and empty.

Alone in their quarters, Izzy spun on Gabe. Her mouth worked, but she couldn't find words offensive enough to describe how appalled she was about their behavior. She whirled away and marched to the closet, yanked her suitcase off the shelf and tossed it on the bed.

Unlatching it, she threw it open.

"What do you think you're doing?"

Ignoring his demand, she began to pitch clothes inside. Then, in a blinding revelation, stopped short. "That's a very good question," she muttered. "These clothes aren't mine. They belong to *Mrs. Parish!*"

"What are you babbling about, Peabody?"

She snatched up the nightgown she'd thrown in the suitcase and turned on him. "I'm leaving in the morning with the other impostors. Good luck on your own."

Clutching the gown to her breast, she dragged her gaze from his, and scurried toward the bathroom. She needed to be alone, take a shower, *feel clean,* at least physically. There was no way on earth she could finish out this fraud. Not remembering the sorrow etched in Hugo's features. Recalling his devastation was like a knife twisting in her belly. She hated herself for agreeing to be a part of Gabe's scheme, however unwillingly.

If Foxie didn't deserve the account, then neither did Gabe. Roger Miles was a good man. Maybe a little rigid but respected in his field. Whatever campaign he came up with would get Hugo back on top. Or, at least, near there. Gabe had a preposterously high opinion of himself if he thought he *and only he* could keep Hugo's baby food empire from collapsing.

Inside the bathroom, Izzy tugged her beaded ivory blouse off over her head and rid herself of her clingy skirt. Casting aside frilly underwear, she stepped into the shower stall. When she turned on the cold water, icy pinpricks battered her. She gasped, deciding her discomfort was a *good* thing. Maybe it would help take her mind off her contempt for herself and Gabe.

She heard an odd sound—a metallic squawk—and turned to see the shower door swing open. "Dammit, Peabody, you can't leave!" Gabe shouted. "I know in my gut we've got this thing—" He stilled, one hand on the shower door, the other clamped around the tile entry. As Izzy tried to cover herself, the angry flush under his skin deepened. "I—I'm—"

"I *know!*" she cut in, flushed with shame. "You're so egotistical, so focused on winning, you didn't *think* about the fact that I would be standing here naked, my privacy violated." She flung the words like knives, trying to keep her wretchedness out of her voice. "Get out, Mr. Parish! I hate the sight of you." She prayed, with time and distance, she could mean it.

Her shock and dismay was mirrored in his eyes, as he realized what he'd done.

She watched his gaze rest fleetingly on her breasts. Even in her rage and hurt, a trembling thrill raced through her. Her anger billowed—but at herself, and her vulnerability to him. *"Get out!"* The demand quivered and broke.

Jaw muscles flexed. "I—I'm sorry...." With a thick swallow, he turned away and closed the door.

So weak she could no longer support herself, Izzy slid to a sitting position. She slumped against the tile wall, her only solid reality in a careening world. The cold water pelted her. She shivered violently, but her physical reaction had little to do with the shower. Drawing up her legs, she hugged her knees. *"Bastard,"* she sobbed, "why can't you see me as a woman instead of a piece of equipment!" She felt so alone, so stupid, so—so invisible!

Her hunger for Gabriel Parish, her pitiful, hopeless

love, gnawed at her heart. She should have left him months ago! "I'm such a coward." She covered her face with her hands. Unable to help herself, she let her tears flow, her sobs cloaked by the shower's downpour.

Gabe lurched out of the bathroom, feeling disoriented and clumsy. He dropped heavily to the bed and shoved a hand through his hair. What in blazes had he done? Where had his mind been? His only excuse was, he'd known Peabody so well for so long, and she'd abruptly announced she was leaving—after they'd come so far, accomplished so much! He'd just—he'd needed to...

Snarling a curse, he rubbed that irritating prickle at his nape. "You walked in on the woman in the shower, that's what you did. *Idiot!*" The memory stirred his blood, and he winced. "My Lord." He rubbed his temples with his fists. "What kind of a self-centered ass are you, Parish?" He closed his eyes, a mistake. All he could see was the vision of her, trembling there, so lovely, so vulnerable, so—so un-Peabody-like.

With a moan, he lay back, staring up, seeing nothing but huge brown eyes, glistening with mortification.

Self-disgust, like the fierce, hot slap of the devil, shot through him. "I'm so sorry, Izzy," he mumbled. "You're right. *Damn* me, I wasn't thinking of anything, or anyone, but myself."

He peered at the bathroom door. He heard the shower running and had a strong sense she was crying. So scandalized by his boorish behavior, she no doubt wanted to die—or, more likely, wanted *him* to.

He lay there staring at the door as though riveted to the bed in that position—forced to watch and wait, unmoving, serving penance for causing her such misery.

What was he going to do? How was he going to convince her to stay? It was true that he wanted the account, but it was also true that he didn't want her to leave him. *Blast it,* he needed her. Why couldn't she see that? Why couldn't she understand how important she was to the smooth operation of his firm? Why didn't she realize she'd found her true calling as his assistant?

He needed the rest of this week to convince her not to quit, not to go off on some half-baked notion about family and children. Ridiculous. What a waste of brains and talent. He clenched his jaws. No. He would not allow her to waste her life, not with her professional competence.

He sat up, determination hardening like a rock in his gut. "Not likely, my little Izzy." He peered at the bathroom door. "You're not deserting me for some nine-to-five bricklayer and a minivan full of cub scouts. Not tomorrow morning, *not ever.*"

CHAPTER SEVEN

BY THE time the shower stopped running, Gabe had concocted a plan. He knew what was best for Izzy, even if she didn't. A little constructive lying and guilt would do the trick. He supposed some people might think he was being slightly underhanded, but he thought of it as merely doing what had to be done. *Blast it*, he was justified, saving his little assistant from herself.

He knew she would take her own sweet time coming out of that bathroom. He'd humiliated her. He wouldn't blame her if she didn't come out all night. He hoped she wouldn't linger too long; he needed her out of there so he could put his plan into action. Deciding he'd better change out of his dinner clothes while he had some privacy, he yanked off his tie and began to unbutton his dress shirt.

He supposed it served him right that the moment he was completely naked, the bathroom door opened. Luckily, he was facing away, standing before his chest of drawers. He stilled, a pair of boxer-style shorts in hand. When he didn't hear the sound of a door being slammed, he peered over his shoulder.

Izzy stood in the doorway, wearing that head to toe black negligee and peignoir. Her lips formed a stunned oh. Her eyes were wide, red-rimmed and bloodshot. He flinched at his handiwork.

In an effort to lighten the mood, he said, "I feel like we've done this before." He grinned. "Only the other way around." He lifted the shorts to indicate his intention to put them on. "I'll just be a second."

She seemed to snap out of her paralysis, for she swallowed. "Oh—I'm sorry, I'll..."

"Don't go." He finished slipping on his shorts. "I'm decent." Turning around he spread his arms wide. "See? If I were in a Calvin Klein ad, I'd be overdressed."

His attempt at humor crashed and burned. Izzy didn't smile. But she didn't slam back into the bathroom, either. Without comment, she rounded the bed and slipped beneath her covers. She didn't seem to notice her suitcase was gone, though he'd put it back on the closet shelf. Of course, she'd made it clear she didn't plan to keep any of the clothes he'd bought her, so it probably didn't matter to her where the suitcase was.

Irritation darted through him, but he tamped it down. He couldn't allow her to see it in his eyes or hear it in his voice. He needed to convince her to stay, not drive her away. He forced himself to settle down. He wouldn't get angry. He would be calm and reasonable—and lie like a rug.

The room blazed with light. Not an atmosphere conducive to sleep, though he doubted she could have fallen asleep that quickly, in any event. Kneading his neck, he padded to her side of the bed and knelt down. Though she didn't stir, he sensed she'd heard his approach and had opted to feign unconsciousness.

"Izzy," he whispered, "Hugo's broke."

Her eyes popped wide and she jerked up to sit. Good Lord, it was as if he'd said "There's a snake in your bed." He had no idea she would react so strongly. Good. *Great*, actually. He needed her to be passionate about this.

"What?" She clutched the sheet to her chest. "That can't be. I—I mean I knew he needed to boost sales, but, I didn't think—I'd hoped it hadn't gone this—far...." Her features were pinched and wretched; her reddened eyes glistened with new tears. *Fine, Gabe, old boy! Humiliate her, then stomp on her heart. That's straight out of How To Be A Bastard—Volume One.*

"He told me about it at our meeting, today," Gabe improvised. "This campaign is a last-ditch effort to pull everything out of the fire." He watched her solemnly, letting the pause do its work.

She chewed on her lower lip. A tear skittered down her face to tremble on her chin. Gabe called himself names he was sure Izzy would be in complete agreement with, if she found out what a devious scumbag he was.

"Why did he tell you?" Her voice was so weak and quivery he could hardly hear her.

He shrugged, as though clueless. "He confessed it after I'd told him my concept."

She blinked, jarring loose another tear from its insubstantial perch on her lower lashes.

He allowed the silence to germinate and grow. *Let her work it out for herself. She has to do the deciding. Or at least think she's doing it.* While he waited, he shook his head as though regretful. The pit of his stomach grew sour with his duplicity.

"But—but his house, the plane, how can he—"

"Mortgaged to the hilt, and he's behind in his payments." Gabe wondered if there was a special place in Hades for men who commit the sin of manipulating softhearted women into doing something that disgusts them—even if it's for their own good. If there was, his spot was assured with this load of horse manure.

He let out a long, theatrical exhale for good measure. "He's such a nice old gentleman. It's a shame." He began to count slowly to ten. He figured since she was smart and compassionate, she'd be ripe for the picking about then.

Eight, nine—

"Do you think he told you because he instinctively felt your campaign would turn things around?" Hope rang in her voice.

Bingo!

"Do you think so?" Consummate jerk that he was proving to be, he managed to sound convincingly startled. "You know, you could be right." He manufactured a small smile, as though appreciative of her brilliant deduction, then quickly banished it. "It's too bad Hugo has such strong opinions about marriage, fidelity—and liars."

She sank to an elbow and brushed at a tear with the back of her hand. "Yes." Her voice was breathy, sad. "It's a silly stipulation." She cast him a solemn glance. "I mean the marriage thing, not fidelity. I certainly agree with Hugo, there."

Gabe said nothing, just kept his expression sympathetic.

"I wish I could do something to help," she murmured, more to herself than to him.

His lips quirked, but he quickly got his features under control. "But you're leaving."

She lifted her gaze, her expression closing in a frown. "Oh, dear." Gabe's jaw hardened as he watched her slide into his trap. "I *can't*," she said through a moan. "I can't leave. Not now." She shook her head and presented Gabe with the most forlorn look he could ever imagine seeing, except possibly from a stray puppy. "I think he confided in you because he sensed your approach was the one that could save his company and all those jobs."

Gabe contrived a look of surprise. "It could be, I suppose."

"Of course, it is." She sniffed and cast her glance to the bed. "Okay—for Hugo..." She sighed, long and low, making it clear she was as happy about this as a convict being told his release had been canceled. "I'll stay until the end of the week." She peered at him for a tick of the clock. "But I *won't* like it."

He pursed his lips in an attempt to mask his satisfaction. With a grave nod, he stood. "If you think it's best."

She lay back, but didn't meet his eyes. "I'm still quitting."

He experienced a spike of frustration. With effort and a count of five, he stifled it. He'd won a battle, but not the war. Not yet. "I understand." Turning away, he walked out onto the balcony. Allowing himself a quick smile, at last, he inhaled the night breeze. He had the reprieve he needed. Now he was sure to get the account. And by Monday morning bright and early, he'd have his assistant back at her desk, too.

He peered up at the nearly full moon. The round, yellow orb seemed to glower down at him. Unperturbed, Gabe winked, feeling better than he had since he'd set foot on Tranquillity Island. "You can't make me feel guilty, old man," Gabe murmured. "What I did was *right*."

* * *

Izzy's mood hovered between gloom and shame all night. As she lay awake, watching golden fingers of dawn move across the sky, she wished she were joining Foxie and Claudia on their trip back to Miami—however disgraced. She hated what she and Gabe were doing, but she was so crazy about Hugo and Clara, she couldn't stand to see their idyllic world crash down around them.

Hugo's life had really only begun a decade ago when he'd married Clara. He deserved happiness. Not to mention the fact that the livelihood of many, many families depended on the Yum-Yum company.

Well, darn it! Izzy was not going to fail them. She knew Gabe Parish well. He might be a workaholic and ruthless at times, but as an advertising executive, he couldn't be faulted *or* surpassed. His campaign would save everything. She knew that in the deepest part of her. She only hoped there was time left to get it into motion.

Unfortunately that wasn't her most urgent problem. Her immediate dilemma was the fact that she had to go on being the fake Mrs. Parish all day, today, tomorrow and part of Sunday. Then—*finally*—she could get on with her life.

Besides, she'd made a vow to help Gabe loosen up, become less shackled to his career. Since his presentation was over, it would be an easier task to accomplish. She just had to be very, very careful she didn't get herself into a situation like the one in the ocean when he'd almost kissed her. The last thing she needed was to add the taste and feel of his lips to her list of Things I Need To Forget About Gabriel Parish.

She closed her eyes and rubbed them hard. Speaking of things she needed to forget, she hadn't been able to erase the sight of Gabe's nudity from her mind's eye. "I didn't need *that*," she muttered.

"You didn't need what?"

She jerked to face the door of the bathroom as he strode through; his wet hair glinted in the golden morning light. Good grief, he looked like one of those superheroes in the cartoons—larger than life, taller, broader, his teeth flashing white starbursts whenever he smiled. She stared, transfixed. Did his teeth really flash, or was her mind playing tricks on her?

To make matters worse, he wore nothing but a towel. She hefted her glance to his face.

"Izzy?" He cocked his head in query. That dastardly grin flashed again. "What didn't you need?"

I didn't need this! her mind shouted. *I didn't need to see you all fresh-from-the-shower-sexy, barely decent in that skimpy towel! That's what I didn't need, buster!*

He continued to smile, but the tiniest frown developed between his brows, as though he were concerned she might have had a seizure of some kind and could no longer speak. She knew she must look like an utter nincompoop, lying there gaping. *Answer him!* she scolded. *Say something!*

"Your legs." Horror skidded through her when she heard what she'd said.

"My legs?" His frown deepened.

Heavens! What had she said that for? *Stupid question, Izzy! You know exactly why you said it. He has great legs!* "Uh—*four eggs!*" It was lame but it would have to do. "I thought I wanted four eggs for breakfast, but I changed my mind. I don't need the cholesterol."

His smile dimmed. He was definitely concerned about the state of her mental health.

Deciding she'd better change the subject, she threw back the covers and bounded out of bed. "It looks like a beautiful day."

"I'm glad you're in a better mood this morning."

She faced him and her manufactured smile faded at the sight—all that contoured, male flesh gilded by sunlight. Unable to deal with so much gorgeous bare skin, she gave him a narrowed look. "Do you realize, you're wearing a towel?"

He glanced down at himself, then back up at her. "Yes." His grin grew wily. "Do you want it?" He made as if he was going to untie it.

"Touch that and I'll scream!"

His grin flashed again, the bum. "I'll bet you say that to all the boys, Miss Peabody."

Her cheeks burned. "I am *not* a prude if that's what you're suggesting."

He ambled to the dresser and drew out some underwear, a knit shirt and shorts. When he faced her again, his grin was still in place. "Personally I like prudes."

"As the main course or dessert?"

"Midnight snack." He winked. "They're delicious, drizzled with chocolate syrup."

If she'd been blushing before, she had to be purple now. Plainly it was his opinion that prudes with purple complexions were hilarious, for he laughed out loud.

Indicating the bathroom, he said, "I'll just be a minute."

"Must you?" *The teasing rat! She'd drizzle him with a chocolate baseball bat!*

*   *   *

Gabe looked at himself in the bathroom mirror and frowned at the stranger staring back. What had he been doing out there? Coming on to—Izzy? *Peabody!* He'd meant to say *Peabody*. He jerked on the tap water and splashed his face. That's not what he was here for. That's not what he wanted of her. "Professionalism, Parish." He splashed, again. "She isn't one of your weekend flings." She was the woman he wanted to keep in his employment, and quickies with employees were not only a bad idea, but they could also create sticky lawsuits. Sexual harassment was nothing to be sneezed at.

He straightened and watched the scowling stranger stare back at him. "You need a woman," he muttered. "But not *that* woman." He stared sternly into the reflection of his own, green eyes. Silently he counseled, *Hold your libido in check for seventy-two more hours, man. In New York you have a little black book full of lusty evenings waiting to happen.* He inhaled, filling his lungs to capacity. His nape prickled and he rubbed it.

Catching a glimpse in the mirror, he noticed his reflection didn't portray a happy man. With a raw curse, he hunched to splash more cold water on his face. He had a gnawing feeling it was going to be a long seventy-two hours.

That afternoon, after a game of croquet on the lawn, Izzy and Gabe returned to their rooms to rest and get ready for dinner. Hugo had told them they would have "a dipsy-doodle of a surprise" that night. Izzy wondered what Hugo's idea of a dipsy-doodle might be?

She hoped, whatever it was, it hadn't unnecessarily drained his coffers. They didn't need all this fluff and fuss. She supposed Hugo needed to do things this way, not so much to keep up appearances, but because his zest for life obliged him to live every moment to the fullest, and that included providing his guests with the same rich experiences.

Once in their room, Izzy exhaled heavily. "I hope he didn't go to much expense for our dipsy-doodle surprise."

Gabe lifted a gift box tied with red ribbon from the bed. "I think we're about to find out." He handed the big white package to her. "This has your name on it."

When she took it, she noticed another box on the spread. It was smaller, but with the same bright red velvet bow. Gabe picked it up. "This little one's to me. I knew he liked you better."

When he grinned, her stomach went all fluttery, drat her! *Drat him!* Trying to return to sturdier emotional ground, she focused on his gift box. "Let's find out what dipsy-doodles are." She laid her package on the bed and untied the ribbon. There was no wrapping paper, so she lifted the lid. When she saw the contents, she giggled with delight.

She drew out a lei of pink orchids, then a hula skirt. A flowered halter top made of a bright, pastel floral cotton was all that remained nestled within the tissue. "Oh my...." she said, excited. "It's a luau!"

"He definitely likes you better."

Gabe's amused tone made her turn. He'd opened his gift. She peered inside the tissue. There were more orchids and more flowered fabric, only the colors were brighter than hers. Curious, she lifted out the orchids. They were fastened to a crown of vines. She bit her lower lip to keep from showing her amuse-

ment. *A crown of orchids—on Gabriel Parish's head?*
Clearing her throat of a threatening titter, she carefully laid the crown aside and lifted out a brief, flowered piece of cloth.

"Tell me it's a napkin," he said.

Izzy burst out laughing, though she shook her head
and waved her hand, trying to communicate she
couldn't help it. "You'll look—very nice." She managed to say it almost without the quiver of a giggle.

"Why do I get the feeling it's not my dinner napkin?"

"It's a lavalava," she said. "Very masculine men
have worn them throughout Hawaiian and Samoan
history."

He stared at her speculatively. "You think this is
cute, don't you?"

"Extremely." Good old Hugo. She couldn't have
thought of a better way to get Gabe to loosen up than
getting him to step out of his polished wing tips into
a lavalava! As each day passed, Izzy grew more and
more crazy about Hugo and his whimsical approach
to life.

Her glance lingered on the scrap of cotton and her
heart did a little flip-flop. She wasn't sure seeing Gabe
in that brief bit of cloth would be a good thing—for
her, at least. After seeing him naked last night, she
knew the less of his flesh she saw, the better.

Suddenly very drained, Izzy sank to the bed.

"Anything wrong?" Gabe asked.

She shook her head. "I think—I'll wash my hair."
Maybe standing under another cold shower would
help.

"Your hair looks nice the way it is."

She glanced toward the sound of his voice. He'd

moved and now stood in the double-doored entry to the balcony, backlit by bright daylight. His arresting looks captured her, and she felt her heart being squeezed as though by a cold fist.

Why couldn't he be her real husband? Why couldn't the loving things he'd said and done this past few days be true? *Because the world does not revolve around the dreams and desires of Isabel Peabody, that's why! Face it, and deal with it like an adult!*

She shoved up to stand. "There's no need to pay me pretty compliments when we're alone—Mr. Parish."

She dashed for the bathroom. When safely inside, she collapsed on the vanity stool and hunched over the cool marble counter, burying her face in the crook of her elbow. She remained there, motionless, for a long time—too broken and bereft to cry.

CHAPTER EIGHT

THE evening was turning out to be more fun than Izzy could have imagined. On the downside, the full moon was too disturbingly romantic for her peace of mind. Even so, she was pleased to see Gabe getting into the spirit, or at least appearing to.

Izzy was a little less enthusiastic now about Hugo's whimsy where Gabe's costume was concerned. He was so elementally male in the scanty wrap, knotted at his waist. Even with the crown of orchids he was almost too sexy to bear. She kept having flashes of a fantasy she couldn't banish, with Gabe sweeping her into his arms and stealing her away to some tropical hut where he made wild, wonderful love to her.

"Flying fish paté?" She was startled out of her musings when Hugo swept a silver tray in front of her nose. Blinking to get it into focus, she saw an artful display of little biscuits spread with a brown-gray matter.

She smiled at her host, trying to keep her sadness at bay. The sweet man always acted so bright and unconcerned. But she knew the awful truth. "Thanks, Hugo. They're delicious." She took one and smiled her thanks. "But I can serve myself, really. Sit down and enjoy yourself."

He guffawed. "I am, dear girl. I am." Hugo then bounded away to offer the tray of goodies to Roger and Hedda. They waved off Hugo's offer of food with such dispatch it irked Izzy. They could have at least tasted it—for Hugo's sake.

The poor repressed couple looked miserable. Roger wore a flowered Hawaiian shirt and white shorts. Mrs. Miles sat ramrod straight in a muumuu, splashed with oversize, psychedelic tropical birds.

Since Izzy had never seen either of them in any colors but navy and brown, she knew they must have been appalled to discover they were supposed to wear the kaleidoscopic garments tonight.

On the other hand, she loved her grass skirt. The way it tickled, skimming over her legs, how festive it was. Most of all, she enjoyed the obvious pleasure Hugo got out of seeing his guests in the spirit of the party.

Hugo was barefoot, like Gabe and Izzy and Clara. The Mileses had not been able to forgo their footwear and looked comical. Roger wore navy dress socks and sturdy oxfords, his wife, hose and brown, lace-up walkers. Izzy's lips twitched at the absurd sight, but she got herself under control. Laughing would be unkind. The poor inflexible dears were suffering to the point of distraction. They hardly touched the delicious roast pig.

"Okay, Izzy," Hugo called, drawing her gaze.

He held a hand toward her. "Come hula with me, girl."

She experienced a momentary pinprick of hesitation, but quickly got over it and pushed up from her wicker chair. "I'd be delighted."

She tramped across the warm sand to where Hugo stood, clad in a longer version of a lavalava, six leis around his neck, and a crown of pink orchids drooping over one eyebrow. Grinning, Izzy took his hand.

He led her to an area before the slithering surf, where everybody would have a good view.

"Okay, ladies and gentlemen, you are about to experience the world's greatest hula dancing team in their inaugural stage show!" He held Izzy's hand high. "When we're finished, I believe throwing money would be appropriate." He squeezed her fingers and released her. "I said, money, remember, not food."

He whispered to Izzy, "You're a good sport, dear girl. My plan is to shimmy and gyrate and act like I know what I'm doing. But I figure if you wiggle, nobody will notice me."

She laughed. "You give my wiggle a lot of credit."

His chuckle was like a squeaky gate. "I calls 'em like I sees 'em."

He threw her a kiss and then signaled his little band. The drummer began to beat out a rhythm. A few bars later, the three instrumentalists launched into a chant. The sound was very Hawaiian.

With a quick intake of breath for courage, Izzy began to undulate her hips and make miming gestures with her arms and hands. Hugo hadn't asked her, but she knew some Polynesian dance basics. Izzy's cousin, Lou Anne, lived in Hawaii. Most summers when they were kids, Lou Anne visited, and taught Izzy something new about the native dances. Since Lou Anne's marriage several years ago, she hadn't visited the mainland, so Izzy was surprised she'd retained so much. Thanks to Hugo's relish for life, she was rediscovering a pleasure she'd all but lost.

As she swayed to the native beat, Izzy was conscious of where Gabe stood, away from the light, leaning against a tall palm tree that arched out toward the sea. He'd left his chair beside her and wandered over to the heavy-laden buffet table a few minutes before Hugo's invitation to dance.

Every so often, as she danced, she found herself peeking into the shadows to see if he was still there. He was. He stood very still, his legs crossed at the ankles. Once or twice, he reached up to knead the muscles at the back of his neck.

After a few minutes Izzy noticed Hugo was no longer dancing, but had stepped away, giving her the stage. She was so startled, she stopped, but Hugo threw up his hands, flicking fingers toward her. "Go on! Go on! You're poetry in motion."

She blushed, but resumed the dance.

Gabe watched her from the shadows, taking in the sexy sway of her hips. The undulating grasses teased with erotic flashes of pale, well-formed thigh. He reached up and rubbed the tingling flesh at his nape. *Dammit,* he'd seen Izzy's thighs before. She'd worn shorts, even a bathing suit. She had great, er, good thighs, there was no denying that.

But there was something different about seeing those thighs taunting him from behind that heaving, pulsating skirt. Something provocative that did things to him. Hot, unruly things. Things that made his mind wonder to diversions he shouldn't consider carrying out with an employee.

She did a subtle pelvic thrust, its effect on Gabe far from subtle. He pursed his lips, let out a low, whistling exhale, then went back to massaging his neck.

Grateful when she was able to stop, Izzy did a little curtsey and scurried toward her seat. Gabe had re-

turned to lounge in the chair beside hers. She hardly
noticed the applause—except his. And his smile.
There was something different about it, quite charming as always, yet with an element she hadn't seen
before. Couldn't quite define.

He stood up, grinning that strange grin and looking
unforgivably sexy. He seemed both amused and ad-
miring. Not the fake admiration he'd paid her all
week, but *genuine* admiration. The significance halted
her in her tracks, and she stared into his eyes.

He stopped clapping and took her hands in his.
"That was quite—something," he said softly.
"*You're* quite something."

She stared in wonder as he winked then bent to
brush a light kiss across her lips.

What Gabe had in mind when he kissed her was a
thanks-for-sticking-this-out-with-me gesture. What he
got was a taste of something he instantly knew he
wanted more of. *Now.* Without the messy interference
of thought, he slid his hands from her fingers up her
arms, drawing her against him. Once more, his lips
found her mouth. This time the act was no fleeting
gesture, no tempting tidbit, no pretense. This time
Gabe kissed her with an eagerness he hadn't felt in—
Hell, he had no idea how long, and he didn't want to
waste time thinking about that, either.

His only thought was how beautifully kissable her
lips were. On their own, his hands slid from her arms
to her back, pressing her into him. Her flesh was hot.
Hot. He'd never thought of his competent little assistant as having hot skin. Peabody wasn't hot. But
Izzy—Izzy sizzled.

He sensed resistance somewhere, and realized her hands were pressed against his chest. He heard a slight whimper deep in her throat.

Good Lord! What in blazes was he doing? Abruptly he lifted his face from hers. She opened her eyes, and without a word lay her cheek against his chest. The act looked like one of affection, but it was a sham. He saw the glimmer of hurt in her eyes, and felt the tension thrumming through her body. Casting a glance around at the gaping onlookers, he forced himself to grin.

"Oops," he said. "I forgot where we were." Another embarrassing truth, but it worked.

Hugo began to clap, and Clara followed suit. Gabe slid an arm around Izzy's shoulders and gently squeezed—a silent apology he would verbalize once they were alone. Hugo cuffed Gabe playfully on the jaw. "You young husbands. You're so full of vim and vigor." He touched Izzy's chin, lifting her gaze to his. Gabe experienced a twinge, witnessing her deep humiliation, though her expression no doubt appeared to the others as shyness, or mild embarrassment.

"I tell you what," Hugo said, yawning so big Gabe knew it was theatrical. "I'm getting tired. What say we call it a night?" He passed Gabe a secret wink, the meaning so unsubtle Gabe could have been one of the folding chairs and still understood its significance. Their host was giving them a graceful out so they could go back to their room and make love.

Though far from happy, Gabe winked back. He knew once Izzy and he were alone, there wasn't going to be any lovemaking. More like a lethal glare from big, brown eyes and a swift kick to the groin.

*   *   *

On the way back to the mansion, Izzy couldn't form a coherent thought. Gabe walked slightly ahead of her, his fingers entwined with hers as he tugged her along. A servant carrying a Tiki torch escorted them, so anything she might have wanted to say couldn't be said.

In her fuzzy-headed state, Izzy decided this threesome was for the best. Having a stranger along helped, somehow. She wasn't sure what emotions might take hold if she and Gabe were alone while her feelings were still so raw—whether she would burst out sobbing, slap his face or cling to him, begging for his love. She recoiled at that last thought. Her mind was throwing out gibberish. She had to get herself on track.

Her gaze slid to Gabe's hand, holding hers. She didn't like the counterfeit intimacy, but knew their ploy required such seemingly trivial contact. At least being led home like this, she could squeeze her eyes shut in mortification whenever the memory of Gabe's kiss hit her full force.

Shutting her eyes didn't really help. She could still feel all the hot, scary sensations she'd felt when his lips claimed hers—warm and gentle, yet with such thrilling boldness, she had no strength to protest. She'd longed for—*ached for*—the touch of his lips for so long, she was helpless. His for the taking. The dizzying caress of his lips had made her weightless, and she'd floated toward heaven, cloaked in a warm glow.

She could do nothing, wanted nothing, but to drink in the joy of his nearness, to know the riotous delight of his kiss. The experience had been so sensual, pure, yet deliciously wicked. She grew light-headed and her heart rate soared to dangerous levels as she relived her body's wild reaction.

She stumbled, the memory making her legs spongy and insubstantial.

"Are you okay?" Gabe sounded as solicitous as a devoted husband should.

She nodded, but didn't meet his gaze. The servant stopped and dropped back to walk beside her so she wouldn't miss another step. Izzy straightened her shoulders and began to mentally recite the alphabet. She had to keep her mind off Gabe and his kisses.

She was thankful, at least, that one fragile thread somewhere in her brain had managed to make her lay her hands against his chest and press, however weakly. Another instant and the ruse would have been blown when she passed out in a lump on the sand.

"Maybe that would have been better," she muttered.

When she realized she'd drawn Gabe's concerned glance, she shook her head. "Nothing—never mind." The unhappy truth was, fainting would have given away more about her feelings for Gabe than she dared allow him to know. She bit her lip. *Would this crazy nightmare ever end?*

The instant the door to their room closed behind them, Gabe let go of Izzy's hand. "I promise that won't happen again." He gently grasped her shoulders and turned her to face him. "I shouldn't have kissed you. It was a mistake." His lips parted, as though he would say more, but after a few seconds, he frowned, and spread his arms wide. "Take your best shot."

She stared. He was *sorry* he'd kissed her. If she could have been any more depressed, that would have done it. Shoring up the cracks in her heart, she lifted her chin. She thought about making a flip comment, but realized her voice would give away her despair. Instead she spun toward her dresser.

"Izzy…"

She reflexively stopped. Her heart fluttered foolishly in the waiting silence. When he said nothing more, she forced herself to move, retrieve her nightclothes and escape to the bathroom.

By the time Izzy came out, she noticed Gabe had turned off the lights and was lounging in his chair. Even though her eyes weren't adjusted to the darkness, moonlight poured in from the open patio doors, allowing her to see him. When he turned her way, she averted her gaze, but she felt him follow her progress around the bed. As quickly as she could, she slipped beneath the light sheet.

"Izzy…" The sound of her name made her jump. Clamping a hand over her mouth, she stifled a gasp. "It's crazy to leave that peignoir on over your negligee every night." His voice was low and edged with irritation. "It's too warm."

She refused to respond and closed her eyes, willing herself to sleep. Several heartbeats later, the creak of his chair told her he'd sat forward. She could almost picture his pinched brow, his hardened jawline.

"Look, I know I haven't been the most gallant Knight at the Round Table this week, but I'm not a slobbering pervert." There was a momentary pause. If he expected her to respond, he had a long wait. "You could be lying there naked under those covers and I wouldn't lay a hand on you."

That's just fine! she threw back mentally, *pour salt on my wounds!*

A drawn-out silence loitered like an unwelcome vagrant. Finally she heard his irritated exhale. "I've been sleeping in this damnable chair night after night, haven't I? That should make my intentions clear."

"Your intentions toward me have *always* been crystal-clear," she said, then snapped her mouth shut. She didn't want to be drawn into conversation with him.

"Then take off the peignoir. Leave it at the foot of the bed. You can snatch it back on at first light. I swear on my mother's head, I won't attack you during the night."

"Don't make fun!"

His low chuckle was far from jolly—more like frustrated. "I'm not making fun."

"Yes, you are."

"Okay—maybe a little." He paused. "Honestly, I can't think of another person in the world I'd forgo sharing a comfortable bed with—except you."

Her throat closed and she blinked back tears. He had no idea his remark was like a knife in her heart. The reaction was ironic and pathetic. She should be grateful he didn't want to share her bed. The single kiss at the luau was going to be hard enough to forget.

"Actually I'm starting to like sleeping in this chair."

He waited, no doubt giving her the chance to take the bait. She bit her tongue to keep from asking why.

"I doubt if I'd sleep in that bed, even if you begged me."

"Don't worry, I won't." She flinched. *Darn the man for having the ability to make her talk to him!*

"Besides," he went on, sounding almost chipper, "sleeping in this chair has been a character-building experience."

"You need one."

"Excuse me?"

Even though she knew better, she repeated, "I said, you *need* one."

His mellow laughter held a hint of real humor. "Don't hold back, Izzy. Tell me how you really feel."

She shifted to peer at him. He sat slightly forward, hands clamped on his knees. His grin glittered in the moonlight.

"Don't you want to know how sleeping in this chair has built my character?"

She knew he was manipulating her, trying to distract her into forgetting her anger. *Not likely, buster!* "I'm not speaking to you!" She hoped a direct statement would shut him up.

"Being in this chair has made me strong."

"What do you do, bench-press it all night?" Darn her mouth! She hadn't given it permission to speak.

He leaned back, steepling his fingers before his lips, his features reflective. More like ninety-five percent sexy and five percent reflective. "I may get rid of my bed." He sounded as though he was thinking aloud.

"We're not having this conversation."

"On my Long Island property, at the bottom of the cliff that leads to my beach, there's a pile of rock. I may take to sleeping there."

"I hope you're enjoying your monologue, because I'm not listening."

"Add a little hail and hurricane winds, and you won't believe the character I could build."

Exasperated that he wouldn't take even her most flagrant hints to keep quiet, Izzy came up on one elbow and eyed him with aggravation. "Maybe you'd better get up and move around. I'm afraid you've cut off the blood flow to your brain."

An easy smile played at the corners of his lips. "I could be the new poster boy for the U.S. Army. Me and this chair—on billboards all across America. They'd get rid of that old, gung-ho slogan about how macho military men do more before nine in the morning than most people do all day. The new one would go something like, 'You can be more uncomfortable before nine o'clock in the morning...' yada-yada-yada." He winked, looking boyish and roguish at the same time. "I'd nail it the first minute of the photo shoot."

Her lips twitched and she grew annoyed with herself. A few minutes ago, she'd been content to wallow in her gloom, but now she found herself fighting an urge to leap into his lap. Drat Gabe and his infectious charm! Well, she wasn't going to fall into his little trap.

"Oh—good night!" The finality of her words idled there in the quiet for a long time while Izzy hardly breathed. For some reason she sensed the other shoe hadn't dropped. She waited, for exactly what, she didn't know.

"Izzy, take off the damn peignoir."

She started, though he'd spoken quietly. He used the same stern tone he had that time she was sick at work. She'd tried to pretend she was fine, but he'd taken her by the shoulders and marched her into the bathroom to look at herself in the mirror. She'd been flushed, her eyes shining with fever—so unmistakably ill she hadn't been fooling anybody.

Admonishing her for being a stubborn nitwit, he'd sent her home in his private car. Gabe didn't suffer fools easily. Right now, she had a feeling he was fed up with her stubbornness. Though she didn't like to admit it, she was roasting.

Heaving a harassed sigh, she shifted to her back and stared up at the wispy canopy. "Will you keep *quiet* if I take it off?"

"Absolutely."

She pushed up and threw her feet over the side of the mattress. Eyeing him with ill humor, she untied the bow at her neck and shrugged out of the thing. Tossing it to the foot of the bed, she clambered back in and clutched the sheet beneath her chin.

"Good night, Izzy."

She squeezed her eyes shut, vowing she would *not* acknowledge him. She would pretend he wasn't there, pretend she took no more notice of him than he did of her. Most importantly, she would *never* admit she was much cooler without the peignoir. She had no intention of giving him the satisfac—

"Thank you..." he whispered.

Deep in the night, Gabe lurched awake, catching himself before tumbling out of the chair. He ran a hand through his hair, trying to clear the fog from his brain. What had jarred him awake?

He heard a sharp cry and realized it was coming from the bed. *Izzy?* He scanned her. She lay in the middle of the mattress. It was obvious from her centralized location, she had slept fitfully, and was fitful now. She cried out, the sound forlorn and breathy. She lifted a hand, reaching, possibly pleading. She mumbled something but he couldn't make it out.

Fearing she would rouse the house, he got up and padded to the side of the bed, unsure what to do. "Izzy?"

She flailed, rolling from her back to her side and then to her back. Her features were distorted with agitation. She reached up, her fingers beseeching, grasping. She yelled out, louder, sharper. Fearful her laments would draw concerned visitors, he slipped into bed and took her in his arms, trying to quiet and comfort her. He had no doubt that her bad dream was a direct result of what he'd put her through.

"Shush." He slid an arm beneath her and drew her close. "Don't cry, Izzy," he crooned. "It's okay." He stroked her hair, soothing her. She whimpered, an arm skimming across his chest and around to his back. It startled him when she held on.

"Please…" She cried softly. "Please—don't—don't…"

Her words became indistinguishable moans, and Gabe impulsively brushed her forehead with a kiss, cuddling her close. "It's all right, Izzy. Don't cry. I'm sorry…" He felt like the worst kind of rat, and stroked her cheek. "I'm so sorry." The things she'd done for him were so far above and beyond the call of duty—*damn*.

He owed her. No wonder she wanted to quit. He'd taken such advantage of her. Well, he planned to make it up to her. He would offer her stock options, double her salary, and never get her involved in anything even slightly underhanded again. She was too principled a person to let these kinds of shenanigans roll off her back—even if it caused no harm.

He held her gently, cursing himself for the bastard he was. After a few minutes she quieted, but continued to hold him desperately. He knew he should leave, but he wasn't sure if he could extricate himself without waking her. He shifted, attempting to pull away, but she wailed in protest, the muscles in her arm tightening. With little choice, Gabe settled back. He nestled her cheek against his throat and rested his chin on top of her head. *A little longer,* he told himself. *I'll just stay a little longer.*

He could feel her breath tickle his chest, along with the vaguest caress of her lips and lashes. Snuggled into the harbor of his body as she was, he couldn't help being aware of feminine curves and valleys, fitting themselves slyly against his body. It was as though some fiendish conspiracy was afoot to mock him with the knowledge that they fit together so well—yet, he couldn't have her. Women, as sexual beings, were interchangeable, but a truly great executive assistant was hard to come by.

Even knowing all that, his recently acquired data about Izzy's physical attributes undermined his pledge not to lay a finger on her. His hands prickled with a contrary desire to—

He fisted his hands. *Remember, jackass, you're comforting her. You've made her life miserable for the past week. Try to think of her needs for a change, and get your mind off her body! In a few minutes, when she's calm, you're going to drag your lecherous butt out of her bed and back into that blasted chair!*

In a few minutes.

CHAPTER NINE

IZZY woke up slowly, reluctantly. She hadn't slept this well in longer than she could remember. Her eyes resisted opening, and would only agree to complete the task in languid little blinks, each one slightly wider than the last, until finally they were reasonably prepared to receive visual stimuli.

She saw lips. Masculine lips. Undoubtedly the most stimulating visual she'd ever perceived upon waking. Those lips seemed familiar. *Gabe's* lips, in fact. What were Gabe's lips doing so close to hers? Confused and muddle-headed, she backed slightly away, or tried to. When she couldn't, she discovered she was enveloped in a pair of muscular arms, her body flush against an exceedingly massive man. A strapping thigh pinned her legs to the mattress.

Coming fully alert, she pressed her hands against his bare chest. "What—do—you—think—you're—doing?"

She watched long, thick lashes twitch, then settle back into stillness. She glared, her mood veering sharply from shock to fury. How dare he cheerfully insist last night that he wouldn't get into bed with her if she begged him, only to find herself tangled up with him in the morning. He had some nerve. Fisting her hands, she shoved with all her strength.

It startled her when he rolled easily to his back. She struggled out from under the weight of his thigh and pushed up from the bed. Her emotions in chaos, she straddled his middle, the flat of her hands on his chest.

She glowered at him, watching his eyes come open. He lifted a hand, as though planning to run his fingers through tousled hair. He looked groggy and cuddly—*the sly fox!* Halfway through finger-combing a stray lock off his forehead, his eyes widened as he registered the fact that Izzy was sitting on his belly. She leaned down until they were almost nose to nose. "What *exactly* is going on?"

She saw momentary hesitation in his eyes, but very quickly a twinkle took its place. "I have no idea." His lips quirked and he finished brushing back his hair. "But it's not a bad way to wake up."

His glib response incensed her. She didn't know which made her most upset, that he'd slipped into her bed on the sly, or that he *hadn't* tried anything. Even allowing such a disobedient thought to flit through her brain made her crazy. "*Ooooooh!*" She fisted a hand and gave him a good, close look at it. "Do you want me to *pop* you, Gabriel Parish? Answer my question. What are you doing in *my* bed?"

His brows dipped, but less in distress than amusement. "Right now, I'm being sat on."

The laughter in his tone didn't bode well for either the length or quality of his life—what little there was left of it. "Don't make me hurt you—you *sneak!*"

She could tell he was warding off a laugh, by the way he pursed his lips. "Look, Izzy…" He took her fist in his hand. "You don't have to punch me to do me damage." He lifted a meaningful brow. "Do me a favor and put on that peignoir."

In one horrid instant she grasped his meaning. Dismayed, she looked down at herself. Bright morning sunlight shining through the thin fabric left little of her body to the imagination. Moaning, she dived for the peignoir. Why did it surprise her that the sleeves were inside out and it took forever to get herself covered. Her face sizzled. The last thing she wanted to do was face him, but she forced herself. She would get a straight answer out of the man if she had to—to—

She inhaled raggedly, glaring with murderous intent. Sadly she had no idea what deadly thing she would do if he decided to plead amnesia. He had sixty pounds on her if he had an ounce.

By the time she got up her nerve to look him squarely in the eye, he was sitting up, lounging on a couple of pillows. He had *some* gall, sitting there like some hedonistic god of pleasure, his arms crossed over a flat belly. He watched her with brows pinched, but no apology was evident in his expression.

"Well?" She crossed her arms over her breasts, giving the sunlight a barrier it couldn't penetrate. "Don't you have anything to say?"

He ran his knuckles along his jaw, and she heard the faint roughness of whiskers. He looked away, then after a drawn-out moment, faced her. "It's not what you think."

His comment took her by surprise. Now she didn't know what to think about *two* things—why he'd climbed into her bed, and what he thought *she* was thinking about why he'd climbed into her bed. She supposed she should be grateful he took it for granted that she had *some* coherent thought on the subject. In truth, she was so confused and conflicted, all she knew for certain was that she wanted to scream.

Working to appear composed, she made stern eye contact. "Tell me what it was, then."

The amusement was gone from his eyes, now quietly magnetic and compelling. "Izzy," he said. "I have never had a more competent executive assistant than you, and I would never do anything to jeopardize our working relationship."

She felt a shiver of disquiet. He was still talking as though she'd never mentioned quitting. "After tomorrow we won't have a working relationship." She lifted her chin a notch. "Therefore, what you just said makes no sense."

A flush spread under the tan of his face, and Izzy sensed it was annoyance at her continued insubordination. He refused to believe she meant to leave him. "Gabe..." Her voice was rough and she cleared her throat. "If I hadn't been positive I was leaving before, you can't think I could stay after—after..." She swept an arm toward him as he lolled in the bed, then remembered she had crossed her arms for a reason and locked them back over her breasts. "After *this?*"

He shoved himself off the bed. With a frown, he mimicked her sweeping gesture. "*This* was not nearly as depraved as you seem to think." He clenched his teeth and exhaled through them. "You had a nightmare and you were crying. I was afraid you'd raise the house so I decided I'd better calm you." His jaws clenched and bunched. "Shoot me for falling asleep. It *has* been a while since I was in a bed."

His dark stare, coupled with the damning pause, forced her to accept the truth. No lust involved—just one part human compassion, one part exhaustion and two parts fear of being unmasked as an impostor.

She felt a hot, foolish rush of anguish. Why else

would Gabriel Parish climb into her bed? Certainly not out of desire! *Are you happy now, Isabel Peabody?* a meddling imp in her brain nagged. *Are you satisfied to know for sure that he didn't come to you in the night because of a carnal urge—like undying love or even mild sexual attraction?*

Gabe checked his watch as he paced back and forth along the balcony. Nearly eight. Time for breakfast, and Izzy was still ensconced in the bathroom. It wasn't that he was hungry, just irritated. He wasn't even irritated at Izzy—well, except for her absurd conclusion-jumping about why he was in her bed. It never occurred to him that she'd go ballistic over a simple charitable deed.

Blast it, he hadn't expected to be in her bed when she woke up this morning. He'd planned to slip out as soon as she was sleeping peacefully.

So why didn't you? he asked himself. *You didn't have to stay in bed, snuggling her against you, inhaling the scent of her hair, enjoying the feel of her curves pressed so sweetly...* "Oh, shut up, idiot!"

"Who are you talking to?"

He cringed. She would have to hear that. Sucking in a breath, he turned, feigning nonchalance. She stood just inside the patio doors, wearing a body-hugging tank top with a lacy insert that only hinted at the softness he'd felt last night. Her shorts were slightly flared and cuffed, showing off way too much leg, now even more delectable with her golden tan.

She wore her hair up. Disorderly wisps skimmed her face and brow. As he watched, a capricious breeze toyed with the airy locks. He watched as though spellbound. How could the motion of a few loose strands of hair sliding from a woman's ear to her cheek be a turn-on? *Dammit, man. You want her! You want to pick her up and crawl back into that bed with her and—and...*

Stalking into the room, he ground out a curse.

"What?" she sounded confused.

Could he blame her? "Nothing." He took her elbow. "Let's go."

"*Ouch!*"

He eyed the ceiling, counting to ten. "I'm sorry." He looked at her and shrugged. "I'm not in a very good mood."

Her expression held visible resentment. "It's a big club, buster." She waggled her elbow. "But it *still* hurts."

He loosened his grip and forced himself to appear nonchalant. "I don't know what's the matter with me. I have no excuse for being testy. I slept fine."

She smirked, but there was no humor in it. "I guess you weren't cut out to be the Compassion Fairy."

He felt the bite of her sarcasm, but made himself grin. "I suppose not. Sleeping with women for benevolent purposes doesn't agree with me."

Her eyes shimmered with contempt. "Odds are, it won't happen again."

Why hadn't he ever noticed how striking she was when she was angry? Maybe because he'd never seen Peabody angry. But Izzy—she was a whole other creature. He rubbed the irritating prickle at the back of his neck. So far, he was batting zero in his plan to keep her in his employment. Things had to change, and change quickly, or he was going to lose her to some construction worker with a barefoot-and-pregnant philosophy. He experienced a sudden, bitter hostility, but kept his expression casual. "Shall we go—darling?"

With a brief nod, she turned those huge, shimmering eyes away and he felt a crazy sense of loss. Visions of that brawny workman running big, calloused hands over Izzy's body—making babies with her—crowded his brain and twisted his gut. Determination clamping his jaws, he banished the image and tugged her from the room. *A woman is a woman. Temporary,* he counseled grimly. *You want to keep Izzy as a vital employee. Don't screw up your game plan by starting to think of her as a woman.*

Late afternoon was set aside to rest and get ready for the evening meal. But today, Izzy had no desire to be trapped in a room alone with Gabe for several hours of uneasy silence and avoiding eye contact. Gabe had acted like a caged lion all day, pacing and preoccupied. She had a feeling the others sensed it, too. Clearly he was anxious for this trip to end. Now that he was almost assured of the account, he'd grown bored with the game. He wanted to move on to new creative coup d'états. The man never paused for an instant to savor his victories or his creations. What a shame.

At the foot of the spiral staircase, she'd excused herself, mumbling she wanted to take a walk. He'd looked puzzled but made no comment, merely nodded and released her hand. Perhaps he was grateful to be relieved of her presence, too.

This way he was free to stalk back and forth in their room, unhampered by her company, as he formulated some grand advertising campaign for his next high-dollar client. She knew who it was, too, for she'd made the appointment. This coming Monday morning at nine. The prestigious Wayfarer Lodge chain. She pushed the thought away. Such things were no longer her concern.

She wandered aimlessly along the manicured lawn, then headed away from the formal gardens toward the tranquil wood. Hooking an arm around a palm tree, she circled it, feeling forlorn. She'd failed miserably in her attempt to get Gabe to unbend, to stop and smell the roses.

She'd been so wrapped up in her own troubles, she had all but forgotten to think of his needs. Finding him in her bed this morning—well, a person could only take so much, only be so miserable, before she simply could no longer be any help to anybody else.

She heard fluttering above her head and looked up in time to see a big blue and yellow bird take wing. Struck by its beauty, she watched the bird as it flitted through the leafy canopy. The parrot flew low and was easy to keep in sight. With a quickened step, and a lightened heart, she followed the graceful creature.

The bird landed on a branch and peered her way, almost seeming to say, "Follow me." She was enchanted by the idea, and when it took flight again, she hurriedly trailed it through the cool, shadowy wood.

Moments later, the vivid bird swooped out of the shade into blazing, golden light. When Izzy reached the spot, she found herself on the edge of the forest. She gazed out onto a quiet cove unlike anything she'd ever seen. Gigantic granite boulders the size of luxury cars were tumbled down on each other, forming oddly shaped chambers, through which seawater whispered and gurgled. Sunlight seeped between lofty crevices and gaps, creating a bewitching show of light on stone and water.

Izzy's heart swelled with appreciation for the quiet beauty of the place. When her feathered guide fluttered into the heavens, she waved him away with her silent thanks. Settling on a warm, flinty outcropping, she watched the water sparkle and surge, watched the tracks of sunlight move stealthily through the chambers of this watery citadel. So quiet, so private. Somehow she felt she had been magically summoned to this retreat as a place of personal healing, a balm to her tattered soul.

She sensed it so strongly, she made an impulsive decision. *Yes!* She was meant to find this lagoon. She would begin her recovering here, embark on a freer existence—start a new life *without* Gabriel Parish or the iron control he held over her days, her dreams and her heart.

For the first time in a long while, she felt sure of herself, sure of what she was going to do, and she experienced the rush of determination to follow through. In one swift move, she tore off her top and wriggled out of her shorts. In another few seconds she'd kicked off her sandals. Wearing nothing but her baby-blue bra and bikini panties, she leapt into the swirling surf with a jubilant whoop.

The water was warm and tingly, massaging her skin. She reveled in the exhilaration of swimming in this little Eden—her secret hideaway for beginning again.

After a time—she didn't know if it had been an hour or more—she spied her parrot friend, perched high on one of the sheltering boulders. Standing breast deep in the water, she waved. "Hello, there."

The bird lifted into the air and disappeared behind the huge stone. Izzy knew if it had flown away she would have seen it, unless it headed directly out to sea. She peered upward, noticing the rock face before her was craggy and filled with fissures and hollows created by rushing currents of water throughout years and years of slow erosion.

Not far above the lapping surface, she spied a gap through which sunshine streamed. Deciding to see if her parrot friend was sunning himself on the other side, she began to carefully lift herself up toward the opening. Being only two feet above her head, she made it easily, peeping out the porthole-size opening. She inhaled the tradewind breeze and smiled. Though the zephyr cooled her body, the warmth of the sunshine made up for the chill.

Finding purchase for her hip, she perched on a stone and leaned against sun-warmed granite. A few clouds scudded across the vast, blue sky. As she scanned the outer surface of the rock, she grinned. Just as she suspected, her parrot friend was there. When she giggled, the bird gave out an ear-splitting screech and flapped his wings. "Ah, *ha!*" She laughed. "You didn't think I could find—*whoops!*"

She felt a jolt and realized one of her feet had skidded off the damp stone ledge where she stood. Reflexively she grabbed an outcropping in front of her, but discovered to her great relief that she wasn't going to fall. Her foot landed on solid rock hardly six inches farther down. Once her adrenaline stopped pumping, she smiled at the parrot. "For a minute there, I thought I was going to crack my skull."

The bird winked at her. The expression looked so wicked she was momentarily flustered, but forced the idea back. "For heaven's sake, Izzy. It's only a *bird!*" Feeling stupid, she waved to her feathered companion. "It's been fun, but I've got to go and get ready for dinner."

The bird screeched again and flapped into the air, as though it somehow understood their time together was over. She shook her head at that weird thought and began her climb down.

When the foot that had slipped didn't seem to want to move, she felt a crawling unease that she might have a problem. Ducking down, she checked it out. What she saw didn't ease her mind. Her foot and ankle had disappeared into a cavity. A chunk of granite, that had cracked off the main boulder, was the culprit. Instead of falling into the water as it should have—if the world were fair—it fitted itself into the hollowed-out shelf, like a lid, though not quite long enough to cover the whole cleft. Her foot was now wedged in the small opening that had been left. Though she didn't dare release her grip on the stone outcropping, she tried to move the chunk with her free hand.

It didn't budge.

She tugged her leg hard to try to dislodge her foot, but all that did was cause pain. She knew enough about such things to realize she mustn't struggle. She would only succeed in damaging the flesh and probably make her ankle swell. She didn't need that.

Settling her hip back on the granite protrusion she'd used as a seat, she hugged the jutting rock at her breast and leaned her cheek on the warm stone of the opening. What was she going to do? She had to think of something. She didn't relish dying this way—practically naked, her foot stuck in a hole. Not only would it be a stupid, embarrassing way to go, but it would put a real crimp in this new, freer life she'd begun.

It took all of Izzy's willpower not to panic, and yank and jerk her foot. If only she had some axle grease, or if a guy with oily hair cream would wander by. She scowled out to sea, watching the sun as it made its slow descent toward the horizon. She wondered what time it was, and had a feeling she should be dressing for dinner. Gabe might be wondering where she was. He might even look for her.

She stiffened with alarm. *No!* She didn't want Gabe to find her like this. She would rather have a battalion of Navy Seals show up. Being humiliated in front of fifty or two thousand sailors—she had no idea how big a battalion was—seemed less harrowing a fate than having Gabe discover her this way. "That makes absolutely no sense, Izzy." She shook her head at herself. Maybe she wanted the sailors to find her because she hadn't found herself in bed with two thousand Navy Seals this morning. And she hadn't had a wild, hopeless urge to have two thousand Navy Seals kiss her until she was giddy.

She groaned. *No!* She would not think about that! Irritated at herself and her turn of mind, she jerked on her leg, cringing at the pain. Bending down, she grabbed her knee with both hands and pulled with all her strength. *"Ouch!"* she cried. *"Get out of there you stupid foot!"* A mighty yank accented each word.

"Need some help?"

Izzy went dead still at the appalling familiarity of that voice. Clamping her bottom lip between her teeth, she squinted toward the craggy shore. Her blood turned to ice. There he stood, legs planted wide, wearing tuxedo pants and shiny black shoes. His knife-pleated shirt was tucked in at his waist, but only half buttoned. *Did he do sexy things like that on purpose? Looking like some Greek god—not quite ready for an elegant Mount Olympus dinner-dance, or more likely preparing to pleasure the Greek goddess of his choice—depending on whether he decided to put on the rest of his clothes, or take them off.* One dark brow rose. His expression was a cross between stunned concern and wry amusement.

Drawing her free leg up to mask as much of her lower anatomy as she could, she pressed her breasts against the blessed outcropping of stone and hugged it with all her strength. Her heart hammered so violently, she wasn't sure the granite would survive. To mask her humiliation, she glowered at him. "Don't you dare laugh!"

"I wouldn't think of it," he said softly, then indicated her with a nod. "What are you doing up there?"

"I'm stuck!"

He swallowed, clearing his throat. Izzy had the most maddening feeling he was stifling a chuckle. "Oh?"

"How did you find me, anyway?" Annoyance sharpened her tone. *Why, oh why wasn't he two thousand Navy Seals!*

"When you didn't come back, I got worried. The gardener said he saw you going this way."

She chewed the inside of her cheek, wishing the gardener would have minded his own business. Of course, if he had, she'd have been stuck there longer. But she wasn't in the mood to be analytical. She was in the mood to cry. She swore to herself she wouldn't and eyed him gamely. "For that keen bit of detective work, I'm sure you'll get your Woman Tracking badge."

He ran a telltale hand over his mouth. The bum! He was laughing! She groaned. "Oh, go away! I don't need your help!"

He cleared his throat again, and started to take off his trousers.

"What are you doing?"

"I'm not ruining these pants. I have to wear them to dinner." He smoothed them across a flat rock.

"You don't intend to come in here, do you?" She hugged the rock tighter.

"It crossed my mind." He shrugged out of his shirt placing it neatly on top of his trousers, then sat down and pulled off his shoes and socks.

Panicking, she tried desperately to come up with delaying tactics. "But—but you'll have to go get a crowbar and grease—and—and—I'm *not* dressed!"

"I guessed that." When he stood, she had another aberrant thought—about how mean it was of Greek gods to look so sexy, even wearing green-and-white striped boxer shorts. "And I won't need anything."

"Oh?" she squeaked. "What are you going to do, *order* the rock to move?"

With a grin he apparently no longer cared to hide, he slipped into the water. After swimming the short distance to her, he stood up. Her trapped foot was chest height for him.

"*No!*" She drew up her free leg more securely. "I don't want you here."

"Shut up, Izzy." He didn't look up, merely examined the situation for a moment before grasping the chunk of granite on the side near her imprisoned ankle. He began to lift. Even in her shattered state, she watched in awe as his biceps and chest muscles bulged with the effort.

"You—you can't—it's too—"

The gnashing sound of stone grating against stone cut off her objection, as the block began to shift.

"Can you get your foot out?" he asked, through clenched teeth.

She tried, and at first didn't think she would be able to, but with a little added tug she popped free. Taken off guard, she lost her grip and tumbled into the water—or to be brutally precise—into Gabe's arms.

She landed with a shriek. When their eyes met, she saw the same shock in his expression as she felt.

"Are you okay?" he asked. "Can you swim?"

"Of course, I can swim!" Her wet lingerie hid little from his view, and she frantically attempted to cover herself. "I got out here, didn't I?"

"I mean, how's your ankle?" His voice was strangely hoarse. "It looks like it's bruising."

She eyed the leg, then shot him a glance. "It's *blushing!* Let me go. I'm fine!"

The instant she felt his embrace slacken, she launched herself away. As she splashed toward shore, she thought she heard him say something, but wasn't quite sure. It sounded like, "Yes, you certainly are," but she had no plans to stop and ask him to repeat himself.

Mortified, she made a frenzied retreat for shore. "Stay there!" she cried.

He didn't respond, so when she reached the rocky slope, she peered over her shoulder. He was facing the towering stone. "Don't turn around!"

He gripped the rock wall with both fists. "Just get dressed."

After struggling into her shorts and top, she poked her feet in her sandals. "I'm going back," she called. "You can come out, now."

He massaged the back of his neck. "Yeah. You're welcome," he yelled grimly. "No trouble at all."

She heard the mockery in his tone, but couldn't fault him for being put out—having to hunt her down, rescue her from her own stupidity, only to have her run off without even a thank you.

On the other hand, she had rights, too—the right to be mortified and just as much put out because he thought finding her, stuck and wearing only the film-iest covering, was so darned funny! Even worse, he was more concerned about mussing his precious tux-edo trousers than saving her.

With a choked, forlorn laugh, she stumbled toward the mansion.

Her newer, freer life—*without Gabe Parish*—was getting off to a shaky start!

CHAPTER TEN

THAT night at the elaborate farewell dinner, nobody seemed to notice that Izzy had fluff-dried her hair on her way downstairs. After running all the way back from the lagoon, she'd taken a quick shower. Gabe got back not long after her, and as soon as she was decent, exchanged places with her in the bathroom. While she had the bedroom to herself, she'd flung on an indigo chiffon slip dress, glistening with random silver threads.

She slid into silver heels as Gabe reentered from the bathroom, wearing his tuxedo slacks and buttoning his shirt. Pointedly ignoring him, she threw herself into the matching diaphanous jacket with fluttery lettuce edging.

She'd been well aware that he watched her tornadic act with the wry lift of a brow. Thankfully he made no attempt at conversation or remarked on her frantic hair-scrunching as they headed down to dinner.

Dealing with the fancy meal had been a struggle, too, as she worked to put from her mind the reality that less than an hour ago Gabe had pulled her—*practically naked*—from a stupid hole in a stupid rock. Even worse, they were now expected to dance together. She would have to look him in the eye. She wasn't sure she could do it. Not after…

Weak in the knees, she sank down on a gold velvet love seat in a darkened corner of the immense drawing room, hoping neither Gabe nor their host would notice her. All she wanted was an end to this nightmare. She wanted to be back in New York, wanted to get a job at some mid-size company on Long Island, far, far away from Gabe's Manhattan high rise. She needed an easygoing boss who went home to his wife and kids at five every night, so she could start building her new life.

"There you are."

She jumped at the intrusion of Gabe's voice. He held out a hand. "We should dance." He indicated the empty floor with a nod. "There aren't many of us left. And Hugo has gone to a lot of trouble."

She eyed him uneasily. "I don't feel like dancing."

His brows dipped. "Is it your ankle?"

He sat down beside her. The love seat was small, and his thigh pressed against hers. She tried not to let it affect her.

"Does it hurt?"

He couldn't see her legs, since her dress was floor-length, and she'd tucked her feet beneath the bench seat. "My ankle's fine." She removed her gaze to where Hugo was standing before his musicians. "The truth is, I don't want any more to do with you than absolutely necessary."

"Is it because of what happened this afternoon?"

She flinched. *Of course it's because of what happened this afternoon. Are you as thick as a brick wall?* "Whatever makes you say that?" In frustration, she balled her fists in her lap. *"Exhibitionist is my middle name! I spend as much time as possible clinging to rock faces with hardly a stitch on, hoping men will show up and leer at me!"*

"Leer?" he whispered. "I don't recall leering."

She jerked to face him. "You don't *recall*—"

Snapping her mouth shut, she turned away. "You have a convenient memory."

"I didn't leer at you, Izzy."

"Ha!"

"How do you suggest I should have gone about rescuing you, then?"

She pulled her lips into a thin line and cast him a quick, worried glance, unsure of what to say. She clamped her jaws, then peeked, again. Dropping her inspection to her lap, she clasped and unclasped her hands. She had no idea what he might have done differently, but she refused to say so.

"That's very enlightening," he said. "Next time I'll blind myself with a stick, so I won't offend your delicate sensibilities."

Heat raced up her neck and burned her cheeks. "Go ahead and make fun."

His long exhale attested to his aggravation. "I'm not making fun. I'm sorry it happened. I'm sorry I had to dislodge you while you were, er, indisposed. I'm sorry about getting you into this whole scheme, since everything I say or do offends you." He was whispering, but his words were clipped and sharp-edged. "Unfortunately we have the rest of tonight's party to deal with, so *blast* it, woman, if you haven't gone lame, *dance with me.*"

"That's such a charming invitation. How can I refuse?"

She heard his muttered curse. *"Please, dance with me!"*

If he could make a request sound like an order, so could she. *"Please, go away!"*

Out of the corner of her eye, Izzy saw Hugo approaching and noticed the Mileses were waltzing awkwardly around the floor. A quick peep at Gabe told her his last words had been growled through a smile that appeared amazingly genuine. She glanced at Hugo again as he came to a stop before her and held out a hand. "My dear, I hope you're feeling all right. You've looked flushed all evening."

She took his hand and stood, more from a desire to separate herself from the troubling nearness of Gabe's thigh than from an urge to dance. "I'm fine, Hugo."

It surprised her when he didn't sweep her into his arms and waltz away with her. Instead he held his other hand toward Gabe, indicating that he stand. "Come, you two. Dance."

When Gabe stood, Hugo placed her hand in Gabe's, then affectionately squeezed their joined fingers. "I want to thank you lovely people for your indulgence this week. I've had a great time getting to know you and the Mileses. As I already told them, I'll get back with you in a week or two about my choice for the account." He touched Izzy's cheek. "I hope you and Gabe will visit us here, especially after you start your little family." He grinned. "Don't wait too long, though." His eyes sparkled with what Izzy feared were tears. "Take it from a man who knows the hazards of wasting precious years."

Compassion for the dear man twisted like a dagger in Izzy's heart. He'd missed so much driving himself all those years. She couldn't bear lying to him. She wanted so badly to tell him that she and Gabe weren't starting any family. Unable to stop herself she said, "Oh, Hugo, we aren't—"

"Thank you for the kind invitation, Hugo," Gabe broke in. "And the advice." He shot her a brief look, though his smile was in place, his eyes flared a warning. He knew what she'd almost done.

Hugo smiled, clearly oblivious to the exchange. "Forgive me for butting in with advice where I don't belong, but I confess to a fatherly affection for you both." Reaching up, he squeezed Gabe's shoulder. "Now, get out there on the dance floor, you two."

As Hugo ambled away to join his wife, the music changed to a slow and sensual melody. Izzy was taken by surprise when Gabe placed a hand at her waist. When their glances clashed, she made sure he could detect bloodthirsty intent. "He wants us to visit once we've started our *family!*"

Gabe's features grew solemn as he pulled her close. "Dance—*darling*." His lips brushed the shell of her ear, as he repeated, "Just dance."

His breath warmed her hair. His fingers splayed at the small of her back, holding her tenderly as they swayed to music intended for making love. Being held so gently in his arms, knowing it was all a sham, tore her apart.

She squeezed her eyes tight and held her breath as she lay her head against his shoulder. She didn't want to breathe in his scent. That would *not* do. She had enough disturbing stimulation with his touch and the dratted sensuality of the music. She refused to smell him, too.

That was absurd thinking, of course. After a minute, she had to suck in a big gulp of oxygen, which included a punishing dose of Gabe's scent.

"What's the matter?" he asked, apparently having felt her inhale.

"I was holding my breath," she admitted, not sure

why the truth tumbled out so freely. Evidently her lack of oxygen addled her brain.

"Why in hell did you do that?" He drew back to scan her face. "Are you trying to faint so you can have an excuse to leave?"

She deliberately placed her cheek on his chest so she wouldn't have to look at him. "Never mind. It was a bad idea."

"That's putting it mildly," he said. "What were you thinking?"

"I don't want to talk about it."

"Are you allergic to my cologne?"

"I wish."

"What?"

"Nothing."

"Come on," he urged. "Is it me?"

"Okay, it's *you*," she whispered. "Happy, now?"

This time he pressed her far enough away to give her a searching look. "My Lord, Izzy." He looked stunned. "I've driven you to hate me, haven't I?"

She felt dismal and angry all at once. She wished she could lie, tell him *yes,* she hated him, but she was defeated by the glimmer of disquiet in his eyes. He hadn't wanted this to happen. He really did value her—as an employee. The affliction in his expression made her heart constrict. Barely cloaked yearnings welled up like a clenched fist, obstructing her throat. She had a reckless desire to pull him to her and hold him, confess that she could *never* hate him. Silly idiot that she was, *she loved him!*

His dedication to his work thwarted any chance for a real life or lasting love—for him or any woman who made the mistake of caring for him. Even if he could see her as a woman, he didn't think of women as permanent, and certainly not as a potential mate. He never would. She dropped her gaze, praying he wasn't somehow able to read her thoughts. "No—sir…" Her voice was frail, but she managed to keep it from breaking. "I don't hate you. I just can't work for you any longer. Please hear what I'm telling you—and *face* it."

When he said nothing for what seemed like an eternity, Izzy had to look at him, to try to detect what he was feeling, thinking. When she lifted her gaze, he was watching her silently, his expression clouded. Disconcerted by his direct stare, she focused on his chin. Her pulse pounded as she sensed his attempt to lock into her mind, read a less final meaning behind her words. She tried to keep her thoughts blank, fearing he might succeed in discovering the truth.

"I see," he said at last, his jaw muscles knotting.

Izzy sensed that he finally, *finally* did see. But before she could respond, he pulled her close, and resumed the dance as though nothing unpleasant had occurred between them. So much for whatever negative emotion he might have felt. It had been dealt with and put aside.

Izzy made it through the rest of the evening in a melancholy haze filled with awkwardness when the pretense required Gabe to hold her in his arms or look lovingly into her eyes. To his credit—and Izzy's dismay—her counterfeit husband performed the tasks with such convincing tenderness it broke her heart.

Gabe and Izzy hardly spoke the morning they were to leave. As he drove their yellow golf cart toward the tarmac, he draped an arm around her shoulders, startling her. "We look like we've had a fight," he said near her ear. "Smile. And it might not hurt for you to kiss me."

She gaped at him, but managed to grin, if you could call a derisive smirk a grin. "I don't *think* so."

He lifted a brow, distinctly irritated by her willfulness, though his smile didn't dim. She was taken off guard when he brushed a kiss across her lips. Though brief, the contact made her woozy, and she saw stars.

"I've never had so much trouble *kissing* a woman in my life," he muttered.

She sagged against him, hating herself for her swooning reaction. She wasn't a fainthearted Victorian spinster, for heaven's sake! "After you get back to New York, I'm sure your luck will change," she said, sounding strangely out of breath.

"It had better."

The visions flooding her brain stung. Gabe, kissing, caressing other women. The talons of hurtful, hopeless green-eyed jealousy clawed at her soul. With a courage-gathering intake of breath she sat up and faced forward, shoving the images to a back shelf in her brain. Let him have his playthings! She had no intention of becoming one of them—even if he *had* been able to see her as a woman. After today, she would be well out of his life.

Through the trees she spotted the blacktop of the runway. "Thank heaven."

Gabe shifted and she sensed his sharp scrutiny, though he said nothing.

The little band was playing as they drove up and parked. Hugo and Clara were weighed down with a rainbow hue of leis. Each of the departing guests received no less than a half dozen. Izzy knew Hugo considered them all his friends, no matter who finally

got the account. In the real world, the soundness of
his feelings was debatable.

Izzy had the uneasy suspicion that Mr. and Mrs.
Miles wouldn't be well-disposed to remain on
friendly terms if Roger didn't get the account. And
Gabe frankly didn't have time for friends outside his
career. Since she was leaving his employ, she
couldn't keep up a friendship. Especially since it was
based on a lie. So, as Hugo placed the leis over her
head, she grabbed him in a spontaneous hug, experiencing a deep sense of regret that she would never
see him again.

Hugo's cool hands grasping her fingers, drew her
from her melancholy thoughts. "And, Izzy, dear,
Clara and I want you to let us know the instant you
decide on a name for your firstborn. I'm planning to
donate a Fine Arts building to my alma mater, and I
want to name it after the darling child."

Izzy was broadsided. Not only because there would
be no baby, but because poor, dear Hugo was carrying
on with the pretense that he wasn't penniless. "Oh,
please..." Tears came to her eyes and she whispered,
"It's okay. I know—about your—your money problems. You needn't pretend with me."

"My what?" Hugo gawked, as though she'd just
told him his mansion was made of blue cheese and
she'd eaten her room. "Where did you hear such an
outrageous fable, dear? Don't you read *Forbes?* Not
to brag, but I'm only a handful of billionaires below
Bill Gates."

Izzy blinked, perplexed. He must know that could
be easily checked. Yet, he seemed genuinely aston-
ished. *"R-really?"*

Hugo guffawed. "Babies need to eat, my dear. Fortunately for me, many, many choose Yum-Yum.'' He tweaked her cheek. ''Now, don't forget to give me your sweet baby's name, you hear?''

With an overwhelming urge to dismember a certain manipulative, soon-to-be-ex-boss, Izzy made Hugo Rufus one more promise, which was nothing more than a monstrous falsehood. ''I—of course.''

Of all the crazy things! Now a whole *building* at some university was going to be named after a child who would never exist! When she turned away to head toward the waiting jet, she was so furious, she trembled uncontrollably. Deep sobs racked her insides, and she had to battle to keep them from spilling out in keening moans.

She shot Gabe a withering glance. His eyes narrowed slightly, Izzy's only indication that he'd received her lethal communication. On the other hand, his expression could have been due to the bright, morning sunlight. Drat the man! Behind that untroubled facade was this latest bombshell tearing at his gut? Or was he such a shameless rogue he truly didn't care?

''A *building!*'' she cried, drawing Gabe from his dark thoughts. He turned toward her, hardly surprised by the accusation in her eyes. Those were the only words she'd spoken in the hour since they settled into the first-class section for the flight to New York. He studied her dismayed expression and felt a fresh rush of fury. Not for her, but for himself and his blasted egocentricity.

''How was I to know Hugo would consider doing something that nuts?'' He shook his head at the enormity of the mess, and glared out the window.

"I don't know if I can forgive you for lying about Hugo being broke."

He shoved a hand through his hair and clamped his jaws, not trusting himself to speak. What more was there to say? That he was sorry? *Dammit*, he wasn't! He'd needed to find a way to keep her on the island. He'd believed he could use the time to make her change her mind about quitting. He'd been wrong, but he still wasn't sorry. He was angry and frustrated, yes—but not sorry. It wasn't only because he knew he would snag the account by keeping her there. It was more. He'd needed those days. He'd wanted—

"You manipulated me as cruelly as you manipulated Hugo," she said. "You'll probably get the account, too." Gabe heard her heavy sigh. "The world is so unfair."

He closed his eyes. *Unfair? From where he sat the world was abundantly fair. He was paying dearly for his misdeeds. She was leaving him, wasn't she?*

"I wish you all the happiness you deserve, Mr. Parish."

Her sarcasm was so palpable, he felt as though he'd been slapped. "Don't call me that."

"Why not?"

He faced her. "Because you're my wi—" He cut himself off, uncharacteristically off balance. "I mean, after we've seen each other na—er—we've slept together..." He blanched at his bizarre ineptness. *"Dammit.* I mean, women who've slept with me know me well enough to call me Gabe."

"If that's a requirement for membership in your Women-Who've-Slept-With-Me club, I don't care to join. Besides, *Mr. Parish*, we have *not* slept together—in the more notorious sense of the phrase."

Blast it! He couldn't get her to continue as his executive assistant now if he kidnapped her and held her at gunpoint. "I don't care what sense of the phrase we slept together in, don't call me Mr. Parish!"

"Why don't you shout that a little louder? A few people in the tail section might have missed it."

He closed his eyes, castigating himself. What was the matter with him, lately? He didn't make scenes. He didn't snipe at employees. And he didn't *lose*, by heaven! Working to calm himself, he pursed his lips and counted to ten.

He was exhausted. More exhausted than he could ever remember being. "Let's not fight." He glanced her way, trying to appear casual. "I appreciate everything you've done, Izzy. I want you to be... happy...whatever you decide to do." What he really meant was he wanted her to discover she hated any new job she took on. He counted on her running back to him. That's what he truly wanted.

"You don't mean that."

He eyed heaven for strength, then met her gaze. Tears trembled on her eyelashes. She looked so broken and defenseless, a primitive grief rushed through him. He'd done her so much harm, disillusioned her so completely, she had no trust left. Could he blame her? When was the last time he'd been straight with her? A week? An eternity? Was it any wonder she despised him?

He didn't want to face it, would never admit it out loud, but she deserved more than spending sixteen hours a day catering to a belly-crawling, self-seeking hustler—who happened to think the world of her.

"Yes, I mean it, Izzy." He took her hand. "I want

you to be happy." He brushed her knuckles with his lips. "I do."

But blast him, did he? Could he really let her go?

Izzy hurried out of the plane ahead of Gabe, feeling his gaze drilling into her back with every step. She had no plans to go to the baggage claim area, since none of the clothes in those suitcases were hers. But plainly Gabe didn't know this, for when she turned toward an exit, he captured her wrist. "This way."

She pulled from his grasp. "I'm going to catch a cab."

His startled expression had its effect, compelling her to babble on. "Those bags aren't mine. Do whatever you please with them."

His lips parted as though he was trying to think of what to say, the perfect something to compel her to rethink her decision. "Izzy, you're going to give me two weeks to find a replacement, aren't you?"

Her stomach knotted with panic. He knew good and well that had never been her intention. He was stalling, feigning ignorance in an effort to finesse her into staying—first, for two weeks while he remained on his most charismatic behavior, then a month, then...

She chewed the inside of her cheek, hating the hold he had over her heart and mind. Vainly she tried to look away from his hypnotic eyes. After a few tense seconds, she saw a twitch at the corners of his lips. His hand engulfed hers. "Two weeks, then. That's my girl." He tugged her toward Baggage Claim, speaking softly, encouragingly, seeming to be in total agreement with her plans. She was merely delaying her leave-taking for two insignificant weeks, he promised. It was the least she could do. This compromise was only fair.

Only fair?

How ironic, she cried mentally. *You speak of fairness, but are you being fair?* This was supposed to be the beginning of her new, freer life. If she didn't take action this instant she would end up spending her days tagging after a man who didn't care any more for her than for his office swivel chair.

"*No!*" She wrenched from his grip. "You're not doing this to me! I'm leaving." Pivoting on her heel, she stomped away, not daring to look back. Her heart thudded so violently she was afraid she would be knocked to her knees. But she trudged on, determined to seize her chance to grow whole again, to become a person with a *real* life. She deserved the opportunity to live fully, to find true love with a supportive man, bear his children, make a home—*be happy!*

"Izzy!" His voice was husky and low.

The urgency with which he'd said her name alarmed her. He needed her, but not in the way she needed him.

"Don't leave me."

She stumbled, her heart crying out for her to turn around, go back, take whatever crumbs of affection and attention he might throw her way for as long as the fates allowed. But her intellect fought back, and fought hard, struggling against the vulnerability in his plea.

Oh, he was good! He could manipulate his voice, choose exactly the right words, to exploit her emotions. He actually sounded distraught. *Ha!* As if the man could feel such intensity for anything he hadn't created out of his own imagination.

She fisted her hands, steeling herself to resist his cunning with every fiber of her being. She couldn't allow him to lure her back! *Not this time!*

She broke into a run, her heart ripping apart in her breast as she fled from the airport—and Gabriel Parish's life.

CHAPTER ELEVEN

GABE rubbed his eyes as he pushed back from his desk. He slouched into the cushy comfort of his leather chair and steepled his hands. He frowned and tapped his index fingers against his lips. What was wrong with his concentration? In the two weeks since Izzy walked out, it seemed he couldn't come up with any ideas that weren't corny and mediocre. Of course, his clients didn't know that, because he could fast-talk anybody into anything.

He exhaled through his teeth. *Except Izzy. He hadn't been able to get her to budge.* He'd lost count of the messages he'd left on her answering machine, offering her the moon and half the stars, if she would come back. She hadn't returned one call.

Not one.

He felt a surge of ironic amusement. She was one self-contained woman, Miss Izzy Peabody. He couldn't envision her in a hair-pulling, clawing fight, with another woman—over him. He'd been embarrassed to witness such behavior a time or two and found it wholly unpleasant. How ironic that he felt a crazy hunger to see Izzy Peabody, so possessive of him she would scratch out another woman's eyes just to...

He cursed, forcing himself back to reality. He focused on his desk, cluttered with wadded pages with the discarded scribbling of his current account ideas. They were junk.

A small padded envelope caught his eye. He knew what it was, and couldn't imagine why he hadn't disposed of it. Picking it up, he dumped the contents into his hand. A golden band lay there. He remembered slipping it on to Izzy's finger the night before their trip to Tranquillity Island. She'd returned it without even a note.

What did he expect? They hadn't really been a couple. Izzy had simply returned a prop from a part she'd played. Though the metal was cold, it glistened like sunshine, reminding him of Izzy. So cold to him now, yet her memory...

"Are you nuts, Parish?" He tossed the ring into his top drawer. "Get your mind on business. She's gone. Face it."

"Sir?"

He looked up, surprised that his new executive assistant had managed to sneak up on him. Bill Beacroft was the height and weight of a football fullback, thirty-something, proficient and bright. The man had come highly recommended, and Gabe was satisfied with his work. He inhaled tiredly, trying not to add, *but he's no Izzy.* How illogical! How stupid. *How he missed her!*

"What is it, Beacroft?" he asked, disconcerted by his weary tone. Why had the excitement gone out of his work?

"That phone call you've been expecting, sir. Mr. Rufus, line one."

Gabe experienced a twinge of discomfort. Here it was, at last. "Thank you, Beacroft." He lifted a stack of computer printouts. "I've made the changes on these. Get them on the hard drive before you leave."

"Yes, sir."

When his beefy assistant exited, Gabe eyed his phone experiencing an odd hollowness. He knew Hugo was going to give him the account, but he felt no pleasure in it. With a complete lack of the euphoria he thought he'd feel at this moment, he punched the button and lifted the receiver. "Hello, Hugo. How are you?"

"Tip top, my boy. Tip top!"

Gabe sat back, enduring a pang of envy at Hugo's unbounded enthusiasm. Gabe wished some of it would rub off. He was tired of feeling nothing about anything these past two weeks. "You sound good, Hugo."

"Thank you, my boy." There was a slight pause. "You sound fatigued."

Gabe closed his eyes and lolled his head against his leather chair. "It must be the connection," he said with a forced laugh. "I'm fine."

"Ah, that's good, my boy."

Another pause. Gabe wished he could fast-forward this conversation to the end. He wanted it over and done.

"I suppose you've guessed why I'm calling?" Hugo said.

"Yes." A dull throb in Gabe's temples told him he was building toward a granddaddy of a headache. "About that, Hugo—"

"You've got the job, son," the older man broke in exuberantly. "My hat's off to you for that ingenious campaign. If Yum-Yum baby food doesn't fly off store shelves, I'll throw away all my happy shirts."

Weary, Gabe closed his eyes. "I wouldn't want you to do that." The man was so damned cheerful. So damn sure Gabe was an honorable businessman.

Honorable! Recently he'd acquired an ugly habit of bursting people's I-Believe-In-You bubbles with behavior that was anything but honorable.

"What's next, my boy? When do we get our campaign going?"

Gabe stirred uneasily in his chair. "Look, Hugo. There's something I have to tell you."

"There is?" The older man sounded cautious. "What's that?" His tone grew worried. "Nothing's happened to Izzy!"

Gabe made a pained face. This was hell. He had to get it finished, *quickly!* "Hugo, it's like this—I'm not married to Izzy and I never was." He exhaled a quick, harsh breath. "Don't blame her. I dragged her into this dirty business, kicking and screaming. She's a good person."

His lips curled in a sneer of self-loathing. "I'm a lying, cheating rat, and—I can't accept your business." He swallowed to clear the roughness from his voice. "Roger will give you a fine campaign."

The duration of Hugo's silence stretched so tautly Gabe began to worry that the kindly man had suffered a stroke. "Hugo?" he asked. "Are you there?"

"Yes." The reply was subdued, solemn. "I'm here."

Gabe couldn't understand why Hugo was still on the line. Hearing the slam of a phone in his ear would have been answer enough. And it would be completely appropriate, considering what Gabe had done. He clutched the receiver, waiting. If the old gentleman wanted to rant and shout, so be it. He'd earned his wrath. *Bring it on, Hugo.*

"What is Izzy to you?"

The quiet question startled Gabe. "She's—rather, she was my assistant."

"Was?"

"She quit."

The soft roar of the air conditioner kicking in was the only sound in Gabe's world for several trying minutes. "Because?"

Because? What in the hell kind of question was "Because?" Gabe wasn't following. Wasn't Hugo supposed to be reaming him out for the liar and conniver he was? He shook his head, trying to keep in step with the old man's disjointed meanderings. Because? It finally came to him. Hugo was asking why Izzy quit. "She was angry with me for the subterfuge."

"I'm sorry."

Gabe shrugged. *Which* was Hugo sorry about—that he and Izzy weren't married, that she'd quit, that Gabe was a liar or that Hugo was taking away his offer to handle the Yum-Yum account? Whatever, there wasn't all that much to say. "Yeah. Me, too."

"From what I saw, my boy, maybe you should be."

Gabe frowned in confusion. His headache was getting worse, which wasn't helping. What in the world was Hugo babbling about now? "Excuse me?"

"Married to her. Maybe you should be."

There was a soft click on the line as Hugo hung up.

Gabe couldn't believe it. "Hugo? Hello?"

Nothing.

With a perplexed shake of his head, he replaced the receiver in its cradle. What had just happened? Hugo seemed more concerned about the fact that he and

Izzy weren't married than Gabe's deceit. And speaking of that, it didn't sound like Hugo had taken the account away, but naturally—*surely* he would!

The man was eccentric, to say the least. His remark about "Maybe you should be" only confirmed it. Hugo Rufus was very odd. *Deranged,* might be a better word—at least in this case. It was almost as though the old guy was suggesting they were in love.

"Yeah. Sure," Gabe muttered. "She loves me like poison ivy, you loony old coot."

Slumping back, Gabe pressed his fists to his temples. The pounding in his head was brutal.

Izzy couldn't be more satisfied with her new job. Mr. Castle was a darling, portly little man who laughed all the time, doted on his wife and four daughters and insisted that everyone leave the office at precisely five o'clock.

The mid-size engineering firm occupied a two-story brick building in the center of Long Island, fifteen minutes from her apartment. She had so much free time, she hardly knew where to begin in her quest to create her new life.

She'd met several nice men at the office who'd already asked her out. Tonight she and one of them, John Geary, were in Manhattan, dining in a posh restaurant overlooking Times Square. Though it was seven o'clock, the sun hadn't begun its descent. At eight, they planned to go to the Broadway show playing right down the street. Izzy couldn't have been happier.

Well, she *wished* she couldn't have been happier. She smiled at John. He sat across from her at their intimate table, ideally located beside a glass window-wall that overlooked the bustling square. Inwardly she berated herself for not being enthralled with her date. He was tall, blond, good-looking and entertaining. He had an abundance of funny stories, and he seemed intent on sweeping her off her feet.

She tried hard to be swept, but her obstinate feet remained stubbornly glued to the ground. She swallowed and revived her smile. *Time.* It would take time. It had only been a month since she walked away from Gabriel Parish. A month wasn't very long. Six months down the road, she would probably have difficulty recalling his name.

"Don't you like your Chicken Moghlai with Coriander Chutney?"

Izzy was startled, both by the question and the fact that John actually recalled the name of her dinner order. At the moment, she would have been hard-pressed to remember it was chicken. "It's delicious." She jabbed a piece of meat and took a bite, smiling and nodding for emphasis.

As John carried on with his amusing story, Izzy tried to appear more interested. She decided, if her date had any flaw at all, it was a borderline intellectual superiority. She had the impression that in a few years he would be a full-blown wine snob and self-important collector of pop art. But right now, he was pleasant enough dinner company. It was a shame, he wasn't a candidate for the easygoing man she wanted in her life—the man she could build a family with, and love with her whole heart and soul.

"Excuse me, I believe you dropped this."

A chill dashed along Izzy's spine. *She knew that voice.* With a quick intake of breath she jerked around for verification. Her heart soared foolishly at the sight.

Gabriel Parish loomed there, holding her napkin. She grew light-headed as she scanned him, her gaze feasting like a starving beggar. He had such a masculine bearing, a larger-than-life presence. Impeccably dressed, he wore a beige silk herringbone jacket and brown slacks. His shirt was pristine white; his designer tie brought out the gemlike quality of his eyes—a cruel trick of the fabric, or the light, or Gabe's innate ability to dress to kill. Whichever, she was captured by his gaze, held in mute bondage.

"Hello, Izzy," he said.

She was jarred from her stupor by the richness of his voice as he spoke her name. "Oh, hello...Gabe." Gathering her wits as well as she could in the face of his unsmiling scrutiny, she plucked the napkin from his fingers. "Thanks."

He nodded, his attention shifting to her companion. "Aren't you going to introduce us?"

She looked hastily toward her date. "Oh—of—of course." She cleared her throat, stalling for time. *What was his name?* She'd gone completely blank. *She knew it only a minute ago!* She smiled and cleared her throat again, as her date looked at her, his smile dimming.

"Gabriel Parish, I'd like you to meet, uh..." She gave an anxious little cough. Her brain was choked with fog. Bill? Bob? John? *"John!"* she blurted, sounding as though she'd just remembered it, which was the unfortunate truth. "John..." she repeated, then opened her lips to continue with his last name, but nothing came. "John—something..." She made an apologetic face at her date.

He regarded her with mild aggravation for a moment before stretching a hand toward Gabe. "*Geary. John Geary.*"

"I'm so sorry, John," Izzy said, feeling like a worm. The poor man had remembered the whole, long drawn out name of her dinner and she couldn't even recall who he was. "I'm just—"

"Forgetful?" Gabe said, his tone curt. Suddenly she had two men annoyed at her. "I've left you several messages, Izzy. Why haven't you called me back?"

She smiled weakly at her date. "Gabe is—I used to work for Mr. Parish." Turning back to Gabe, she focused on his throat for safety's sake and inhaled to pull herself together. "Thank you for your interest, but I've found a new job."

When he didn't say anything for several troubling heartbeats, she found herself obliged to look at his face. He smiled, then, but his direct stare flared with hostility. "As long as you're happy."

"I love it," she said, too quickly. "I get off at five and it's not far from where I live." *Why can't you just go? Why do you have to stand there driving me crazy, making me want you?*

"Congratulations." He glanced at her date. "I won't keep you. It's nice to have met you, John."

For the flash of an instant, his gaze clashed with hers. A second later he was gone, leaving his heady essence in his wake. Izzy tried not to turn and watch where he went. She didn't want to see his woman du jour, didn't want to know *anything* about him or his love life. But she turned, darn her.

When he joined a tableful of men she experienced overwhelming relief and expelled a pent-up breath she hadn't realized she'd been holding. At that instant, the awful, painful truth rammed her like a truck. She wouldn't be over Gabriel Parish in six months. *Try six years!* a nasty little voice in her head jeered. *Try sixty!*

Defeat pressed down on her, and she found it hard to breathe. The room was suddenly stifling, the air thick. How was she going to exorcise Gabriel Parish from her mind and soul? How could she get on with her new, freer life, if he carried her heart around in his pocket?

Her throat aching with hopelessness, she turned back to her date. Though she was drowning in her despair, she tried to smile. From his pinched expression, she knew he was through attempting to sweep her off her feet.

That, unfortunately, was the least of her worries.

Izzy's heart did a little skip when she saw the broad-shouldered man standing before the elevator in the Castle Engineering building. As she approached, he turned slightly, and her disappointment was harsh and cruel. His profile wasn't even a pale imitation of Gabriel Parish. She hated her fluttery reaction whenever she saw this man, Evan Page, one of the company's senior project managers.

Though the employees dressed casually, Evan looked so much like Gabe from the back, she never failed to overreact when she saw him. She was ashamed of herself for being so foolish. It had been a week since she'd seen Gabe at the restaurant. A long, dreary week, if she allowed herself to admit it. But she didn't. She stuffed it. Only when Evan happened by, did the damning truth claw its way to the surface, making her emotions fly into chaos.

Seeming to sense her behind him, Evan turned around. From the front he looked nothing like Gabe, with his close-set, black-button eyes, wide nose and shaggy mustache that completely hid his mouth.

He grinned at her. She could tell because his mustache canted upward on either side of his nose. "Hi, Iz. Ready for the weekly meeting?"

Working to get herself under control, she hefted her briefcase full of reference material. "I just finished making copies of the weekly project stats for you guys."

Evan checked his watch, and Izzy's attention was drawn to his muscular arms. Evan worked out, and had a nice physique. Why was it that she only appreciated it for how it reminded her of—

The elevator bell dinged, mercifully tearing her from her thoughts. After she and Evan rode up to the second level, they strode between cluttered cubicles toward the CEO's corner office. Equally cluttered, but with two windows, Mr. Castle's office had a nice-size table that would accommodate Izzy and the eight executives who attended these meetings.

Her boss handled the weekly chore of reviewing the status of current projects with humor and easygoing aplomb. She liked him, and didn't mind the meetings, but it was Friday, and she was anxious to be by herself. She had a wild weekend planned— wallpapering her bathroom. It wasn't her idea of paradise, but her bathroom would be happier. She peeked at her wristwatch. Four-thirty. Mr. Castle would have them out of there by five, or her name wasn't—

"Izzy Peabody?"

She stilled, staring at her watch. She must be further gone than she realized. She'd just *thought* her own name in Gabe's voice.

Mr. Castle cleared his throat. "Miss Peabody," he said quietly. "You have a visitor."

Confused, she looked at her boss. He stared in the direction of the door. The room had gone quiet, not a paper was shuffled, not a finger or pencil rapped on the tabletop. Everybody else was staring, too.

She turned slowly, her heart leaping to her throat. *No,* her brain scoffed, *he's not there. It's not him. What would he be doing out of his office at this hour?* Yet, even though she knew it couldn't be true, her breathing seized in helpless anticipation.

When she saw him, she couldn't believe it. Who was this man who looked like Gabe Parish *from the front?* He was dressed casually, like one of the employees, here, in off-white slacks and a green polo shirt. His hands tucked in his pockets, he watched her with a speculative gaze. A green gaze. Just like Gabe's.

"May we help you, Mr. Parish?"

Izzy felt an electric sparkle as her boss said the name. Then she wasn't hallucinating? Mr. Castle recognized him. Apparently they all did. Gabe was well-known enough to be recognized, she supposed. But surely he wasn't here to solicit their business. Mr. Castle couldn't afford Gabe Parish. Besides, engineering firms didn't advertise on TV or in slick national magazines.

"I'd like a private word with Miss Peabody."

She sucked in a breath. Her mind was trying to whisper something but she didn't dare listen. It was too crazy. Too impossible.

"Me?" she squeaked.

He lifted his chin in a half nod. His smile was slight and one-sided. "In private, please?"

"Certainly." Mr. Castle pushed up from his chair at the head of the cluttered table. "No problem at all, Mr. Parish. We were nearly finished." Her boss took Izzy's hand, tugging her to stand. "Go, Miss Peabody. I'm sure we can get along without you for a while."

Bewildered, she could only stare at Gabe. Now that she was standing, she noticed he wore Docksiders, but no socks. Wholly unlike him. Trying to maintain a composed facade, she asked, "Why aren't you at work?"

He walked toward her, his advance masculine perfection in motion. When he drew near, she took a defensive step backward and found herself pinned against the table.

"I'd like a favor," he said softly.

Her senses filled up with his aroma and she had a wayward desire to fall into his arms. She fought it, putting a stern edge to her words. "What's wrong? Are you in urgent need of a wife for another week?"

He did a long, slow slide with his glance, taking in her windswept curls, her summer sundress, her sandals. When he met her gaze again, he took a step closer. "I'm afraid so."

Before she could comprehend what was happening, she found herself swept up in his arms. "And the next week..." His lips against hers startled and delighted and frightened her, but she was helpless to resist. She'd longed for the caress of his kisses, craved the feel of his hands on her body. How many nights had she tossed and turned, yearning...yearning...

"No!" She pushed away, making herself be strong.

"I'm not doing that again, not for all the accounts and awards and ego-boosts in the world." She wriggled in his embrace. "Let me down!"

"Would you reconsider if my request included a home, children and a man who can't live without you?"

"You're not dragging me into any more of your phony—your phony…" She faltered and frowned. Something new had come into his eyes. Something fine and soft and vulnerable. Her brain clambered back over what he'd said, tripping and stumbling, as she tried to make sense out of it. *Home—children—a man who can't live without you?* When she fitted the words together, they sounded very much like…like…

A strange, warm glow filled her whole being, but she didn't dare hope. "What—*what* did you say?"

The sun broke into his eyes, and they shimmered and smoldered at the same time. "I want you to be my wife, Izzy," he murmured. "This week—next week—and on and on. Please, marry me. I want to be beside you as we watch our children grow up, then our grandchildren and our great-grandchildren."

In numb astonishment, she stared at him. Millions of tiny bubbles began to burst and pop and fizz inside her head. Tinny noisemakers quickly joined in the fanfare. The clamor was deafening—like New Year's Eve in Times Square. She shook her head to try to quiet the brouhaha. Why couldn't she think straight? What had he said?

"Izzy, I've known for years you were indispensable to me. I just didn't understand how indispensable—until you left." He brushed his lips against hers. "I love you."

She heard masculine ahs and ohs all around them, but she was too stunned to care.

I love you!

"You—you actually said it," she whispered in wonder. "Out loud. In front of witnesses…"

To her!

Glistening, earnest eyes searched hers. "Is that a yes?"

She relaxed her guard. Sinking into the cradle of his arms, she breathed in a deep, soul-quenching draft of air. "Oh, yes. *Yes,* darling. I've loved you—for so long."

His smile was as intimate as a kiss. "Then we'd better go. If I remember correctly, you want a large family."

An instant later, she was being whisked away.

"Miss Peabody is resigning," Gabe called over his shoulder. "I'll send you a temporary replacement. He's very good."

Nine months and three days later, on a pleasant March afternoon, their first daughter was born. That summer the Dora Isabel Parish Fine Arts building was dedicated at Hugo's alma mater, and afterward little Dorie and her mommy and daddy visited her godparents on their island paradise. In short order, so did baby number two, three, four and five. All happy, healthy Yum-Yum infants.

Along the way, Gabe came to understand what was truly meaningful in life—his wife, Izzy, and the children they created together in their unwavering love for each other, and their passionate joie de vivre.

Harlequin Romance®

REBEL Brides

Two rebellious cousins—and the men who tame them!

Next month **Susan Fox** brings you a stunning sequel to **To Claim a Wife.**

Sparks fly as Maddie finally meets her match in the irresistibly gorgeous Lincoln Coryell!

Look out in July 1999 for:

TO TAME A BRIDE (#3560)

Maddie St. John is everything **Lincoln Coryell** dislikes in a woman—she's glamorous, socially privileged and devotes all her time to looking good! But when they're unexpectedly stranded alone together, Linc sees a whole new side to Maddie—and realizes he could be the man to tame her!

Available in July 1999, wherever Harlequin books are sold.

HARLEQUIN®

Makes any time special.™

HRRB

If you enjoyed what you just read,
then we've got an offer you can't resist!

Take 2 bestselling love stories FREE!

Plus get a FREE surprise gift!

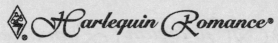

Harlequin Romance®

We're proud to announce the "birth" of a brand-new series full of babies, bachelors and happy-ever-afters: **Daddy Boom**. Meet gorgeous heroes who are about to discover that there's a first time for everything—even fatherhood!

We'll be bringing you one deliciously cute **Daddy Boom** title every other month in 1999. Books in this series are:

February 1999 **BRANNIGAN'S BABY**
Grace Green
April 1999 **DADDY AND DAUGHTERS**
Barbara McMahon
June 1999 **THE DADDY DILEMMA**
Kate Denton
August 1999 **OUTBACK WIFE AND MOTHER**
Barbara Hannay
October 1999 **THE TYCOON'S BABY**
Leigh Michaels
December 1999 **A HUSBAND FOR CHRISTMAS**
Emma Richmond

Who says bachelors and babies don't mix?

Available wherever Harlequin books are sold.

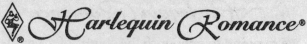

Harlequin Romance®

**brings you four very special weddings to
remember in our new series:**

WHITE WEDDINGS

True love is worth waiting for....

Look out for the following titles by some of
your favorite authors:

August 1999—SHOTGUN BRIDEGROOM #3564
Day Leclaire
Everyone is determined to protect Annie's good name and ensure
that bad boy Sam's seduction attempts don't end in the
bedroom—but begin with a wedding!

September 1999—A WEDDING WORTH WAITING FOR #3569
Jessica Steele
Karrie was smitten by boss Farne Maitland. But she was
determined to be a virgin bride. There was only one solution:
marry and quickly!

October 1999—MARRYING MR. RIGHT #3573
Carolyn Greene
Greg was wrongly arrested on his wedding night for something he
didn't do! Now he's about to reclaim his virgin bride when he dis-
covers Christina's intention to marry someone else....

November 1999—AN INNOCENT BRIDE #3577
Betty Neels
Katrina didn't know it yet but Simon Glenville, the wonderful doctor
who'd cared for her sick aunt, was in love with her. When the time
was right, he was going to propose....

Available wherever Harlequin books are sold.

HARLEQUIN®
Makes any time special.™

Harlequin Romance®

Coming Next Month